ISBN 0-910043-19-1
This is a special double issue of *Bamboo Ridge, The Hawaii Writers'
  Quarterly*, issues #48-49, ISSN 0733-0308.
Library of Congress Catalog Card Number 90-85158
Copyright 1990 Darrell H.Y. Lum
Artwork copyright 1990 Arthur Kodani
Some of the work in this collection has previously appeared in
  Bamboo Ridge, The Hawaii Writers' Quarterly, *Seattle Review*,
  Chaminade Review, *Hawaii Herald*, *Landmarks*, and *Hawaii Review*.
Published by Bamboo Ridge Press
Edited by Eric Chock with Gail Harada, Wing Tek Lum,
  Rodney Morales, Cathy Song and Holly Yamada.
Managing editor: Cathy Song Davenport
Cover and book design: Susanne Yuu
Cover art and other artwork: Arthur Kodani
Typesetting: Beau Press

————

Bamboo Ridge Press is a non-profit, tax exempt organization
formed to foster the appreciation, understanding, and creation of
literary, visual, audio-visual and performing arts by and about
Hawaii's people. Your tax-deductible contributions are welcomed.

Bamboo Ridge Press is supported in part by grants from the State
Foundation on Culture and the Arts (SFCA). The SFCA is funded by
appropriations from the Hawaii State Legislature and by grants from
the National Endowment for the Arts. This book is also supported in
part by a grant from the National Endowment for the Arts (NEA), a
federal agency.

Bamboo Ridge Press is a member of the Coordinating Council of
Literary Publishers (CCLP).

Subscriptions to *Bamboo Ridge, The Hawaii Writers' Quarterly* are
available for $12/year to individuals and $16/year to libraries and
organizations.

10 9 8 7 6 5 4 3   93 94 95

Bamboo Ridge Press
P.O. Box 61781
Honolulu, Hawaii 96839-1781
(808) 599-4823

Acknowledgments

Thanks to the members of the writers group who have nurtured and supported this book. And to my family, immediate and extended, for these are their stories. And thanks especially to Mae, Lisa, and Daniel for their love.

—for my father, who told me stories

Contents

BOOLY
Waste time...
You get dollar?
What you think dis is? Bank of Hawaii?
Burrito's tooth came out... he put it under his pillow...
10 cents enuff...
ZZZZ
But it was his buck teeth!
OK den... got da dime?
Oh, about 9 o'clock

NO PASS BACK

I hate Alfred. He so stupid. Everytime he catch it from everybody and jes because him and me get da same last name, da guys all tell dat he my bruddah. But he not. He get da same last name as me but he stupid and he kinda fat and when he breathe he make noise wit his nose and his mout. J'like one horse. J'like he always stay huffing and puffing. J'like he no mo nuff air.

Nobody like be Alfred's friend. Nobody like be his partnah. Nobody like even talk to him, except me. I gotta cause I sit next to him. I gotta sit next to him because da teacha make us sit alphabetacal.

I everytime gotta give Alfred one false crack because somebody go play Pass On, No Pass Back. Dey punch you in da arm and den tell, "Pass on, no pass back." So you cannot crack um back, you gotta pass um on. I tink Benjamen Funasaki da one dat always start um. Den it go down da line: to da G's, and den da H's, and da I's, no mo J's, an den to da K's. Get plenny K's: Kim, Kimura, Kodama, Kodani, and den come da L's. Get plenny of dem too: Lau, Lee, Loo, Look, and den Lum. I can tell get one false crack coming when I hear somebody tell, "Ow!" and den you hear, "Pass on, no pass back." And when get to me, everybody stay waiting. So I gotta punch Alfred and tell, "Pass on, no pass back."

Da ting is dat Alfred no pass um on. He jes look at me and den he put his head down and den he cry. He no punch back or nutting. He no pass um on.

One time I went try tell him dat he gotta pass um on. Ass how you play da game. But he no like. He say he no like punch nobody.

Alfred like hang around by me even though I no like hang around him. But sometimes I gotta. When Benjamen and John play basketball and dey choose up sides, always get me and Alfred left over. We da substatutes. We gotta jes watch from da side wit da small kinnigahden kids. Or when Benjamen and John choose up, one side gotta take us two guys fo one good guy. Not even one real good guy, jes one medium good guy. Us two fo one. Den me and Alfred, we gotta watch da behind part . . . waay behind.

One time at recess, Benjamen and John went make like dey had ooh-gee germs and dey went wipe um on Alfred and den push him inside da girls batroom.

"Ooh-gee germs," dey went yell. "Pass on, no pass back!" And all da girls went tink dat Alfred was going try get dem so dey went run outside screaming, "Ooh-gee Alfred going touch you!" But he only wanted to get back outside. Da Campus Patrol went nab him and den report him fo going inside da girls batroom. Alfred nevah say was Benjamen and John dat wen push him inside. He had to pull weeds recess time for one whole week fo breaking da rules. But was j'like he no care. He jes went by where da janatah told him fo go and he went pull weeds and catch beetle bugs in da dirt.

Pretty soon, all da kinnigahden kids went come by him fo watch his beetle bugs. He went make one house fo da bugs in da dirt. Had one yard wit one rock fence and one old milk carton wit water fo da swimming pool.

When da janatah wasn't looking, Alfred went give da kids horsey back rides, too. Da small kids grab anykine fo hold on: his hair, his ear, his nose, his eyeglasses. But Alfred no mind. He jes laugh and go until da tetherball pole and come back.

Pretty soon da kids was lining up fo ride Alfred every recess dat week. Dey nevah like watch basketball no mo. Dey jes went wait their turn in line and watch da beetle bugs. Benjamen went come by Alfred's bug place fo look what was happening. One beetle bug was coming by him and he went try step on um but da small kids all went push him away, even though dey was scared of da beetle bug too. Benjamen went tell one small kid, "Try come, try come." And da kid went come and Benjamen went punch um and tell, "Pass on, no pass back," and den run away.

All da kids started fo do dat, Pass On, No Pass Back, and everytime got stuck at Throw-up Shirley. Throw-up Shirley, she always throwing up. And she wasn't too good at playing Pass On, No Pass Back so dat everybody knew already dat when she came by you, she had to pass on one punch. So pretty soon everybody jes run away from her and she little mo cry until Alfred went tell, "No do dat," and he gave her one ride two times around da tetherball pole.

Next time, Alfred was absent so one kinnigahden kid started fo bahdah me fo give him one horsey back ride. "Nah, nah," I went tell um, "I stay substatute fo basketball." Den Benjamen went come by me and ask me if I like play basketball fo his side. Da small kids was scared of him. Dey thought he was going give dem one mo punch.

"Nah, I no like play," I told Benjamen, "I gotta give dis kid one ride." Funny, I nevah feel like playing basketball dat time. I dunno why. Den I went *hapai* da kid, carry um, you know, and we went around da tetherball pole and den came back. J'like how Alfred do um. By da time I came back, had one line.

Da next day, was all bus up, Alfred's bug place. Da kinnigahden kids went cry but Alfred went make one grave and had j'like one funeral and all da small kids went put flowers and leaves on top and Alfred went make one cross out of sticks. Maybe I should have told him I seen Benjamen by his bug place las time. Maybe Alfred already went know. I dunno.

Alfred no need pull weeds anymore but he still go by his bug place every recess time. Da small kids tell, "Yea!" when he come. I wish he wouldn't do dat. Now I da junkest guy. I da only substatute and cause dey no can choose up with him and me for one good guy — two fo one — Benjamen and John no like me play wit dem. Well den, I no like play Pass On, No Pass Back either. Nowadays I no hit Alfred when da ting come around da G's, da H's, da I's, da K's and L's. And Susan, she sit right before me, most times she no pass da punch on to me either. Even when Bennett punch her hard. Bennett punch everybody da same, boy or girl, he

blass um. But once, I seen him and he nevah
punch Susan when was Pass On, No Pass Back.
Hey, j'like we passing um back, yeah?

VICTOR

The sugar cane was tall and thick. Almost time for harvest, Victor thought. It'd be nice to stop and chop myself a stalk like Uncle Manny taught me years ago; he chose the dark, thick, almost purple stalks and chopped them into foot-long pieces. The tough, fibrous cane provided hours of sweet chewing and even more hours afterwards of picking cane fibers from your teeth.

Victor thought he saw something flit across the road. He flicked the wheel to swerve and braced himself for the thud of hitting an animal but there was none. He checked the rear view mirror. Nothing. Nothing but small, furry animal carcasses littering the roadside.

The car was loaded with water jugs, lantern fuel, food, and books. Everything he needed for two weeks of solitude in Mike's cabin. The Ozakis were the last pioneers; Mike and his wife Jenny lived on seven acres of woods above the canefields. The access road belonged to the sugar company and the front chain link gate was usually locked. Someone had to make the three-mile drive down from the cabin to open the gate whenever they had visitors.

It was a hard life. Jenny refilled the jugs for their drinking water every day when she drove down the hill to teach at the high school. And it seemed incongruous that right outside the gate was one of the island's largest suburban districts, a planned community of nearly identical three- and four-bedroom homes complete with wall-to-wall carpeting, underground power lines and running water. The red dirt of the area, full of iron oxides, once sustained acres of cane fields and their accompanying field mice and rats. With each new increment of development, the cane, the mice, and the rats were driven further up the mountainside.

The cabin was actually a pole house dug into the side of the mountain, a solid three-bedroom home anchored to telephone pole-like logs bolted to concrete footings. Pole houses could be built on practically any terrain and were especially suited to these steep mountainside lots where it was nearly impossible to excavate a level lot. The house had a view on three sides and the wrap-around lanai took full advantage of this. Quiet. Private. Views from every room.

The last time he visited, Victor hadn't noticed that when the wind blew, the whole house creaked and shuddered, then settled itself back down with sudden groans and ticks. It was hard to imagine something so solid would move at all. But it did. He supposed it was the wind sweeping across the valley floor and up the side of the mountain that caught the underpinnings of the house and caused it to flex. Still, as he peered over the railing, he saw that the poles were securely strapped to the footings. And the concrete footings were reassuringly three feet square, some about six feet deep.

That night, Victor could hear the wind strumming on the long threaded rods that kept the poles aligned. The humming of the rods changed pitch with each gust of wind and at times sounded like voices. He would have preferred the constant hum of the freeway outside his apartment in town.

"I suppose I could get used to even this," he said aloud. His voice echoed in the large, barn-like house. He was surprised at the sound of it.

One day here and I'm already talking to myself, he chuckled to himself. So much for quiet. He felt vaguely uneasy. Restless, he lay in the unfamiliar bed.

Then there was the matter of the pattering of what sounded like feet on the roof. A steady click, click of claws across the shingles in short, rapid bursts. Birds? Mice? Rats? Mongooses? He had heard something all day but like everything else, it seemed amplified at night.

Mongooses. The mongoose was one of those great ecological blunders that changed the natural environment of the Hawaiian Islands. Brought in by the plantations to help control the rat population in the fields in the early 1900s, the mongoose ate the rats only when it had to. It preferred eggs, chickens, and other ground-nesting birds. The rat population scarcely diminished while the complaints from poultry farmers mounted.

Victor remembered taking BB gun target practice on the animals when he was a kid. They were tough. Hitting them square on the side didn't even make them flinch. His brother was into heavier artillery and had used a .22 rifle once. Victor had refused to watch, imagining mongoose guts splattered all over the hedge. His brother later reported that the .22 slug did stop the mongoose, but only long enough for it to fluff its tail and hiss at the inconvenience.

He even remembered trying to catch mongooses to earn spending money. Somebody at the University paid seven dollars per animal, as long as they were alive and unharmed. Victor liked the idea of trapping himself a bunch of the little animals. But although he often saw them flashing across the driveway, his assortment of nooses and boxes and wire traps had failed. He had even armed himself with his father's leather garden gloves and the mango picking pole with the wire hoop and the cloth pouch at the end after he had heard his brother talking about mongoose bites and mongoose rabies. His mother put a stop to his hunting efforts after she discovered that he was using her eggs for bait. He had never gotten rich trapping mongooses.

He burrowed his head into the pillow and listened. It must be mongooses. It must've been mongooses along the road this morning. He had never seen so many dead ones before.

Whoever did them in used more than a .22, he mused. The tapping on the roof seemed more ominous. Mongooses. The sleek, beady-eyed creatures were nothing more than furry snakes with legs. Why had they chosen to congregate around here? What did they used to call them? He tried to remember. Cane snakes? Cane snakes. He fell asleep to the droning voices of the wind through the foundation rods.

It was almost ten o'clock before he woke. The morning sky through the sliding glass doors was cloudless. Pure, deep blue. Victor closed his eyes and remembered the noises of the night before.

I should check around outside the house today, he thought. He heard a click-click on the roof but by the time he opened his eyes, it had stopped.

During breakfast he watched the heavy equipment clearing house lots near the freeway. More ticky-tacky, he thought. He found Mike's binoculars and did a 180-degree sweep from the lanai. There was no wind and the cane was dead still except for the areas immediately around the earth-moving work. He noticed the cane stalks near the edge of the clearing were shivering as if something at the base of the stalks was holding and shaking them. The Caterpillar driver was piling the debris into a little mountain on one side: old, unharvested cane, weeds, and the junk of a forgotten field. The one section of cane seemed to quiver every time he dropped a load nearby. Victor watched through the binoculars as a cloud of black smoke blew out of the exhaust and the rear wheel spun. The big machine slipped sideways and the driver jumped from of the operator's seat clutching one eye. He looked like he was in trouble. Without a phone, Victor couldn't call for help and he was at least ten minutes away down the steep, winding road. He was unable to stop himself from watching the driver's agony. It seemed like the driver was alone. Victor had to go help.

He searched the bathroom for an emergency kit and found some gauze bandages. He tossed some ice into a plastic bucket, then loaded the car and started down the hill.

After one wrong turn, he found the field. A cane company truck was pulled up beside the tractor. Two Filipino workers were pressing a wadded-up tee-shirt against the driver's right eye.

"Hey, what happened?" Victor asked.

"Cane stalk poke his eye," one of them said. "Danger, you know, work by da sugar cane. Da leaf tip sharp. Gotta wear goggles like us when you work by da cane."

"Hmmph," the other worker grunted in a deep voice.

"You called for help?" Victor asked.

"Aye. Call on da radio already. Dispatcher send ambulance."

"Here, I get clean bandage and ice. Maybe make da bleeding stop."

"Yeah," the driver said, "I like ice."

"You okay?" Victor asked, feeling stupid as soon as he had said it.

"Goddamn mongoose," the driver said.

"Mongoose?"

"Yeah. Dey must be piss off that I busting down their place or something. Dey all ovah dis field. Must've been dem, da mongoose. No mo wind. How can one time da cane come la dat?"

"What you mean?" Victor asked.

The driver repeated, "Da damn mongoose know. Dey know! Dey went push or chew up da cane so dat da tall ones fall in front da machine when I raising the front loader. Den da cane went slide off da top of da loader and poke me in da eye."

Victor looked skeptical. "They not that smart. Jes accidental, I tink," Victor said.

"Hmmph," the quiet one shook his head at Victor, "you donno. . . ."

The driver continued, "Yeah, da damn mongoose. Dey know, da vicious little buggahs. Ass not no cute little stuffed animals like dey sell at da tourist trap out on da North Shore. Whachucall? Willy-willy Mongoose? Goddamn little snakes. Alla time dis happen ever since dis project start. All kine little funny stuff. But nobody like believe."

"Hmmph. No good dis kine. Bad luck, though," the worker said. "Everytime around here, dis field, somebody in da crew get hurt. Somebody step inside mongoose hole or get eye poke or mongoose steal their lunch. Bad luck dis field. Nobody like work dis one already. We jes whack da mongoose nowdays. No good. Some even try come bite you. Even me I get one mongoose bite one time. I no do nutting to him and da damn ting come right up and bite me. Dat one I cut off his head and tail," he chuckled to himself remembering the story. "Da supervisor see me and tell me leave um alone. He tell me dey eat da rats, I tell him, 'Dey eat me!'"

"So what you went do?" Victor asked.

"No can do nutting. Only go dispensary and get tetanus shot. Go home for one day. Next time I going drop mongoose balls on his desk!"

"Danger, you know," the other worker added, "I hear you can get rabies. . . ."

Victor turned to tend to the driver, not wanting to hear the rest.

The driver thanked him after the ambulance crew got him packed up and bandaged. "Shoot some of those suckers for me, eh?" he told Victor. Victor took the drive back up the hill slowly. He was spooked. He forced himself to gaze at each dead animal along the side of the road to remind himself that he was ultimately more powerful than the little furry creatures that were not much larger than the rats they were supposed to eat. He wondered how so many of them had died. Some of them might have been done in by that worker; they looked like they had a machete cut along the side of the head.

Those old Filipinos must know. That quiet one who only said, "Hmmph," looked like he could take a few out with his bare hands. His sharp features and sloping bald head made him look like one of the animals he was after. His low, deep voice sounded familiar somehow.

It must be that worker and his superstitious pals, Victor thought as he passed more carcasses. Displaying them on the road probably was their way of making their feelings known to the supervisors. Wonder if they're going to get a "mongoose clause" in the next union contract.

Back at the house, Victor inspected the roof looking for ways that mongooses could get access to the roof. There were a few low branches on an ironwood tree grazing the eaves that might possibly provide access. He found a machete, a rope, and Mike's aluminum extension ladder in the garage. The pitch of the roof was steep and as soon as he was up on it, he regretted being there. He stood up wavering in the wind then dropped to all fours and edged toward the branches.

"Don't look down. Don't look down," he said aloud. The branch was hanging over the roof by about three feet and he stood at the edge to hack away at it.

Now I know why they call these things ironwoods, he thought. It was tough going but the swinging of the machete and the sweat made him forget his fear of the height and the reason he was up there in the first place. He learned to lean into the wind when it gusted and he paused often to look around. He convinced himself that whatever had been clattering around on the roof last night was not going to be clattering around tonight. There was no other way to get on the roof except by ladder or by a long, nearly impossible climb up from the foundation. Pausing to catch his breath, he could make out the field where the accident had happened. He could see the Caterpillar parked haphazardly halfway up the side of the rubbish pile. He wondered how the driver was doing. Hope he doesn't lose the eye, he thought.

Victor cooked himself a steak that night out on the lanai. He cleaned off the grill, scraping the charred remains of the last cookout over the railing. He heard some rustling in the brush below but couldn't see anything. After the steak and a half bottle of wine, he leaned back and watched the streetlights blink on in the subdivisions.

They don't know what they're missing, he thought. This is the life.

He began to understand why Mike and Jenny put up with all the hassles of living up here. It wasn't all that bad. There were all the propane appliances and water from the rainwater tank for showering and washing dishes. Only the drinking water had to be brought in as the water collected in the tank hadn't passed Board of Health inspection. Something about finding animal hairs in the water supply. Victor recalled Mike mentioning the need to go in and scrub the tank before trying to get approval again. He wondered what was contaminating the supply.

Not a bad life after all. I'll clean up tomorrow, he promised himself before going to bed.

He awoke in the middle of the night to the clattering of his dinner plate falling off the lanai table. Looking through the lanai door, he saw what must have been thirty mongooses bickering over the remains of his dinner. He rattled the door to try to scare them away but like his BB gun years ago, it had little effect. They ignored him and went on with their business.

"Shoot um," he remembered the driver telling him. "Shoot those suckers for me." How the hell had they gotten up here? He went around the house, closing windows and checking the screens. He checked all the doors.

Damn Mike didn't tell me about this, he thought. The closest thing he could find to use as a deterrent was an aerosol can of mosquito spray. He edged the lanai door open and sprayed the stuff through the screen door. Nothing. The ones he hit turned to look at him as if peeved that their coats got wet. He shut the door.

Victor remembered the old man's story, "Damn ting went bite me."

Mike really ought to have a phone installed. This is carrying this pioneering stuff too far. If I could only call an extension agent, he could probably suggest something that would get rid of these pests. Looks like they're just interested in the food. Maybe they'll leave when the food's gone.

Victor considered hooking up the water hose to try blasting them off the lanai. But the hose was outside and he wasn't about to open the door to get it. He absent-mindedly washed the stray dishes in the sink, thinking that he should have cleaned the dishes he had left outside. He cupped his hands and took a long drink of water from the faucet then spat it out spluttering and spitting after remembering that the drinking water was in the jugs.

Maybe it was mongoose hair in the water, he thought.

He spent the rest of the night worrying about the mongooses and keeping track of the scraping and clicking noises outside. He tried leaving the lantern on, then off. He considered a flaming torch but couldn't risk setting fire to the lanai or the surrounding forest. He finally gave up and simply drew the drapes and retreated to the bedroom. They hadn't left after fighting over the food. They ended up trotting around the lanai in little packs of five or six like little wolves on the prowl. In bed, he heard them on the roof again. Victor started to make a list of things to do the next day and after he had exhausted the grocery and supplies list and a list of errands, he kept coming back to the first item: Check with extension agent. Poison? Traps?

He fell asleep to the clicking feet of the mongooses and to the droning of the rods, huh-hmm, huh-hmm, huh-hmm. . . .

When the sun eased up over the horizon, he checked the lanai. The animals were gone. The lanai was in shambles and mongoose droppings

were on the floor near the broken dinner plate.
Further down the lanai, there were three dead
animals gnawed with entrails spilled and he
assumed cannibalized. He picked up his list and
headed out the door. Somehow he didn't feel
relieved that they were gone. Remembering the
comfort of swinging the machete, he grabbed it on
the way out. He loaded the water jugs and the ice
chest into the trunk of the car and jumped in. He
headed down the hill. Dead animals still littered the
road. There seemed to be even more this morning.
He drove carefully, avoiding the fresher ones. A
skittering noise in the back seat made him turn to
face a pair of beady mongoose eyes set in a sleek,
tapered head. He flashed on the quiet Filipino man
until the animal perched on the top of the
passenger seat hissed at him and fluffed its tail.
Victor grabbed the machete and swung at the
uninvited passenger. He missed and tore the fabric
ceiling liner of his car instead. The mongoose
hadn't moved.

The old BB gun mentality, he thought. He
hit something and felt a thud as the car swerved to
the side of the road. He jerked the car back on
course and felt another thud. He swung the
machete again, backhanded, and caught the animal
with the flat of the blade on the side of the head.
The thunk of the skull was reassuring. Got um.
Those old guys would be proud of me, he thought.

In front of the car, standing stock-still in the
middle of the road, was yet another one. Victor
headed straight toward it. As he braced his arms
against the steering wheel, he felt the odd
sensation of being watched. Like being in the
center of the stadium with thousands of eyes on

him, hundreds of binoculars being focussed. He heard more than felt the "thump" of impact. The cane was moving in odd ways, against the prevailing winds. He closed his eyes.

Sometimes I feel mean. I like go bust someting. Some guys like bust car antennas but I only like go spray paint. I donno, I feel mean and I feel good at da same time, you know. It bad, but still yet I like spray paint. I donno why. Make me feel mean when I stay painting but feel like I stay doing someting. Someting big you know, so dat I stay big, too. I no paint swear words la dat. I paint my name and make um fancy wit curlicues undahneat. Sometimes I paint my babe's name but I no like do dat too much, bumbye everybody know, you know. Sometimes I paint one surf pickcha. One real tubular wave wit one guy jes making it . . . cranking through, you know.

When you paint on one new wall, j'like you stay da first one in da world fo spray paint. Even if you know get someting undahneat dat you went paint before, when da wall stay new, I mean, when dey jes paint up da wall fo cover da old spray paint, j'like stay da first time you painting. You can feel da spray paint, cool on your hand. You can smell da spray, sting your nose but sweet, j'like. I no sniff, you stupid if you sniff, bumbye you come all stoned and you no can spray good. But j'like it make you feel big. Make you feel good dat your name stay ovah dere big. Like you stay *somebody*.

Coco. Ass my name. "Coco '84" is what I write. I no write um plain, I make um nice, you know. Fat lettahs. Outline um. Wit sparkles. Da kine dat you can make wit white or silvah paint, like one cross or one star. From far, j'like your name stay shiny. I stay undah da freeway aftah school fo watch my wall. I watch um from across da street by da school parking lot. Everybody who pass look at my wall everyday. I try put someting new everytime so get someting new fo everybody to see. Only little bit at a time, like some more lines on da wave or one diffrent color outline on my name, stuff la dat. Jes about everybody look at my wall, even if dey pass um everyday, dey look. Sometimes when get some other guys by me aftah school I no can paint new stuff but da people dat pass still yet try look fo figgah out what stay new.

Aftah school I gotta wait fo my mahdah pau work pick me up. Sometimes I stay by da guys when dey no mo baseball practice la dat but most times I stay by myself. Everyday gotta plan how you going paint. When you paint, you gotta plan um good. You gotta be fast. You gotta know what you going do. And you cannot get nabbed. How many times I almost got nabbed, man.

One time somebody went put "Rockerz Rule" on my wall. Was anykine way. Wasn't nice. Had some guys hanging around da wall and I went ask dem, "You went make dat?"

"So what if we did?" one of da guys went tell me. I told dem, "Eh, I know da guy Coco, and he going bust your head if he find out you went spray on his wall. He big you know, Coco."

Dey went look around first fo see if I had backers. Since nevah have nobody, dey went ack like dey was tough. But finally dey went go away. Dey nevah spray nutting else except fo dis one punk kid went spray and walk. Had one crooked

black line all da way across my wall. I would've
beefed um but I nevah like. I would've given um
lickins. I could've taken um.

Nobody know I spray paint. Nobody even
know I stay Coco. If they knew, they would say,
"Naht, dass not you. I heard Coco stay one big
guy. You too runt fo be Coco." Funny yeah, but
dass me. Ass me, Coco. One time I going paint one
big mural and everybody going know ass me.
Would be good if you no need paint fast and hide
when somebody come. Could make um nice and
people would even buy da paint fo me. I would
make da whole wall wit spray. I would paint faces,
my face ovah and ovah and I would make um look
mean and tough. And I would look *bad* and I
would be feeling good. I would make sparkles and
you could see dem shining in my eyes. I would use
silvah and some black paint. People would tink,
"Who did dat nice one?" Dey wouldn't paint um
ovah. Dey would buy me paint. Dey would gimme
money fo paint da walls all ovah da place.
Wouldn't need to do work in school. Da teacha
would gimme one spray can, not brush and
paypah, la dat. Junk, when you paint in school.
Gotta do certain tings, certain way. No can be big.
No mo feeling. Ass why spray paint mo bettah.
Make you feel mean. And bad. And good.

One time had one lady came by da wall. She
wasn't one teacha or nutting cause she had long
hair and had jeans and tee-shirt la dat. I had to
hide my spray can when I seen her coming. I
nevah like her bust me. But you know what, she
had her own spray can and went look right at me
den she went spray on my wall:

REVOLUTION FOR THE 80'S
MAY DAY.

Den she went little mo down and went spray out my "Coco '84', and went put "WORLD WITHOUT IMPERIALISM, NO IMPERIALIST WARS" right ovah my surf pickcha.

When she was pau she went look at me and say, "You know what dat means?"

"No," I told her.

"Dat means we gotta tell people to fight da government. Gotta get da people together and tell da governments not to have wars. Gotta give da poor people money and food and power la dat."

"Oh," I said. "But lady, why you went spray um ovah da wall? You nevah have to spray um ovah Coco's stuff. You could've put um on da top or on da side or write smaller. Look how you went jam up my pickcha, I mean Coco's pickcha."

"Sorry," she went tell kinda sassy.

"Why you gotta paint da kine stuff?"

"Cause I like. So what, kid." She was coming little bit piss off. So aftah she went go away, I went try fix my wall up. But she went use red. Hard fo cover, red. She nevah have to put um right ovah my writing. I wanted dem fo come paint da whole wall awreddy, erase um so dat could start ovah. I jes went get my can spray and I went stand in front da lady's words. I was feeling mean. Not good kine, jes mean. I went write "LADY — HATE YOU" not nice wit fat lettahs or sparkles but jes anykine way. I nevah care. Was ugly, jes like her's one.

When my mahdah came pick me up, I seen her reading da wall. "Who went do dat?" she went ask me. I told her one lady wit long hair and tee-shirt. I went ask her who dat kine lady was and she went say, "Dat Commanists dat. Not Americans. Hippies." She told me, "Dey good fo nuttings." I was looking out da window when we went drive away. Couldn't even see "Coco" anymore.

I couldn't tink about anyting except what I was going paint ovah da hippie lady's words. First I thought I could paint somemore surf pictures but I went check my colors and I figgahed would be too hard fo cover da words. Da lady, she went write big. I thought I could do "Coco '84" mo big but still couldn't cover da lady's words. Would use up all my paint.

Aftah school da next day, I went to my wall. Could see da lady's words from far away. I jes went look at her spray paint words. Ass all was, jes words. Ugly words dat nobody like read. Not like mines, not nice wit sparkles la dat or curlicues or one pickcha of one surfah in da tube. Jes words . . . anykine words. Everybody going say, "Hoo da ugly. Who did dat?" What if dey tink was me? Betchu da painter guys going come paint da wall fast. J'like the time somebody else went write "Sakai Sucks" and everybody knew dey was talking about Mr. Sakai, da principal. Dey came right away fo paint da wall dat time.

Nevah feel good anymore fo look at my wall. Wasn't mine anymore. Wasn't Coco's. Wasn't even da hippie lady's cause she no care. Was nobody's.

And den da next day had posters pasted up on da wall. Was somemore stuff about May Day and had one pickcha of one guy holding up his fist. Dey nevah only put one, but dey went line um up. Had maybe six or seven or eight all line up. Cover everyting: my surf pickcha, my name, even my "hate you" words. And dey went paste um on good. Dey went use someting dat stick real good to da cement and den dey even put da paste on da top so dat da ting was stuck extra good. No can peel um off. Hardly can scrape um even. Only little bit. I seen da hippie lady aftah school looking at da posters.

"You went do dat?"

"What you tink?" she went tell me.

"I donno. You went do um, eh?"

"So."

"You shouldn't have done dat. Coco going come piss off, you know. Dis his wall. Maybe he might even call da cops or someting."

"Who's dat, Coco? Dat you? Betchu da guy no stay. If he so big, how come he no come talk to me himself? From now on dis is everybody's wall. Not only Coco can paint on dis wall. Anybody can paint. Me. You. Anybody."

She jes went keep on talking, "Eh, you no need be scared of Coco. He ain't so tough. What he going do to you?"

"Yeah but, not supposed to be writing on da walls. . . ."

"Who said? Da government? Coco? Coco went paint first. He went liberate dis wall first time. But now he no can hog um. Dis wall is fo everybody I tell you. Uddahwise he stay making up anykine rules. J'like one nudda government."

"Hah?"

"How come you gotta watch dis wall fo Coco? You jes being Coco's stooge, you know. You shouldn't have to be scared of Coco. Dat's jes like da people who scared of the government. I mean you no need be oppressed by somebody else. . . ."

Couldn't tell what she was saying cause one truck was going on da freeway and from far could hear one police siren. Da lady went stop talking and we went look up at da freeway listen to da siren coming closer. Went pass.

I jes told her, "No paint on top Coco's wall, eh. Or else you going be in trouble. Coco, he big, you know. He *somebody*, you know." She nevah say nutting. She jes went walk away but I was still yet telling her anykine stuff, "You no can jes cover up my wall la dat. Was *my* surfah. Was *my* wave. Was *my* name! I hate you hippie lady!"

I went get my can spray and I jes started fo paint one face right ovah her words. I donno whose face. Jes one face. Was black and red. Had plenny lines in da face. Was one mean and sad face. I jes went keep on adding lines to da face and came mo black and mo black until was almost like one popolo but wasn't. Jes was one face wit plenny lines on um. Da paint went run out when I was fixing up da cheek. Went drip. I couldn't finish um. I went cross da street and watch my face.

Had some guys in one truck, regular fix-da-road guys, went come and look at da posters. Dey took out anykine scrapers and some real strong kine paint thinner fo take da posters off.

"Awright," I went tell dem.

"Damn kids do anykine yeah," one guy went tell me.

"Naht, wasn't kids. Was da hippie lady," I went tell um.

"You know who was?"

"Yeah, da hippie lady who come around here sometimes."

"You not da one, eh?" da man went ask me.

"Nah, but da guy Coco spray."

"Coco spray dis kine words?" Da man was pointing to da word "hate" between da posters. Could only see "lady" and "hate" left.

"Nah, he make nice kine stuff. He no paint ugly stuff."

Dey went clean off all da posters and started to paint da wall.

"What fo you paint da wall awready? Da hippie lady only going paint um again. What fo?"

"At least going look nice fo little while," da boss guy told me.

"Eh, try look dis face," one of da guys went point to my pickcha wit his roller. "Not bad yeah? Look almost like somebody crying wit dis red drip ovah here. You know who went do dis one? Pretty good artist. Too bad gotta cover um up."

I jes went turn around. I started fo cry. I donno how come.

HORSES

It was in beginning sculpture class that Zoo had the feeling return. When they started laying the plastered strips of cloth over his face, Zoo tried to remember the steady slow breathing from kung fu. "Hurry up!" he tried to say without moving his lips. They dipped strips of cloth into a bucket of plaster and pressed them tightly into his features. Someone kept saying, "Get it in good around the eyes and the nose . . . we don't want to have to do this again." When they laid the larger piece of cloth across his chest, he felt the heat of the plaster setting and he began to sweat.

"You're moving. Stay still. Take shallow breaths . . . don't move your chest. . . ." He forgot the slow breathing and ended up taking long pulls of air and holding his breath against the heat and the weight of the plaster on his chest. He had forgotten how his joints ached and how he had to control his breathing so that he wouldn't hyperventilate and how his shoulders and knees stiffened whenever he had to hold still in a particular position. He remembered hot parade days in high school ROTC, how, despite the Sergeant's advice not to lock their knees, cadets and their M-1s dropped in the ranks as if picked off by a sniper. They were felled by the heat and having to stand at attention while the flags passed and the medals were handed out. The two students who had the most demerits to work off had to rescue the fainters: run to each one, grab the rifle and drag the cadet off to the shade until he revived enough to rejoin the ranks before it swept in front of the reviewing stand.

Shoulder to shoulder they turned in tight formation and each platoon leader side-eyed his row for alignment. "Ai-ees height!" Zoo felt their eyes on him as he looked straight ahead, trying to keep his platoon walking straight and in step, calling out instructions under the noise of the band, "Wipe the smiles off, Torres outa step, turn tight everybody, here we go, look sharp." They turned like a line of circus horses, strutting to the heavy drumbeat of the band, the ones on the outside taking long strides, the ones on the inside marking time.

"Lay-ft, lay-ft, left-right, lay-ft."

The feeling would surface years later in a little girl's complaint about her ballet teacher, Mrs. Kimura, who made them stand holding their plié until she came down the row of little ballerinas correcting their body, feet and arms. And being the smallest and the newest she was last and always fidgety by the time the teacher came around. She complained that her arms hurt from holding them up so long and why couldn't she put them down until teacher got to her. Her father would be nervous as they faced Mrs. Kimura the next week to explain why she wasn't going to be coming anymore. "Wait a minute, I'm the customer here," he'd remind himself, but still he felt nervous and would have to smile a lot. He would make small talk to make it seem like the kids these days couldn't seem to stick things out. But he knew that the little girl was right. Mrs. Kimura would look at him, expressionless. Such a weak father. The child needs discipline. Who is the parent here? Finally she would say, "But she is getting better . . . don't you want to try a little longer?" Mrs. Kimura knew to appeal to the child and not the father. They would walk back to the car, defeated it would seem.

Teacher, sergeant, *see foo*, *sensei* . . . it was all the same. And now people would stand in front of this sculpture, perhaps years from now inspecting it, judging it, examining the position of the hands and arms, this sculpture looking like a moment frozen, the faces surprised. They would check to see if you could tell that it was actually made by trapping people in plaster and making them breathe through straws in slow, controlled breaths. Could they detect the panic rising in his gut?

And still years later, it would be the same little girl in parent/child karate class who worried about her dad standing in the back row with all the other parents, mostly fat, middle-aged ladies. Could he touch his toes? Could he do twenty push-ups? Could he remember all the steps? Please don't turn the wrong way! When you take the test, do you have to go up with your parent? What if the kid passes and the parent doesn't?
"Quit turning around and checking on me," he would have to tell her finally. "Sensei is watching you. He'll make you do pushups."
It was the same feeling . . . the tightness in the joints. The knees ready to buckle and always the pushups. Pushups for being late, pushups for not paying attention, pushups for conditioning.

"Thank you Sensei, for making us do pushups!"
they shouted each time. And when she quit he
would not be there. She had to face Sensei alone
but not before she would earn her blue belt. He
would still feel the racing heartbeat and the ache in
his joints as if he were there. "So why did you
even come if you were going to quit?" Sensei's eyes
would ask.

Perhaps it was his family's propensity to
arthritis — severe debilitating bouts with knobby,
swollen joints; hands and elbows and knees
gnarled and lumpy like some Halloween witch —
that caused the ache. A look at his mother and all
his uncles and Zoo knew that trying to negotiate
the world with hands that could close only halfway
was all he could hope for in his old age. Or would
it be the hidden pain of hip joints calcified or the
pain of the loss of control of everything he loved:
pens, pencils, a keyboard, the remote control to the
TV, his Nikon.

"Een-spec-shun harms!" Slap the webbing
strap, slap the stock, push open the bolt until it
clicks and hope it doesn't snap shut again. If the
platoon did it right, there were three distinct
sounds: the click of the metal fastenings as you
slapped the strap, the fleshy slap of hitting the
oiled, wooden stock, the metallic slide and snap of
the bolt being pushed open. You tried to do this in
three counts and not wobble afterwards from the
effort. If you were a hundred twelve pounds, a
twenty-pound rifle is almost one-fifth of your body
weight and if you were left-handed, your right
hand bore most of the weight. Sergeant Lima
wanted everything sharp, snappy. If you were

quivering and sweating, he'd just take that much longer to inspect your weapon. Stick his thumbnail into the chamber and peer down the barrel looking for lint before thrusting it back, no, tossing it back to you, so that if you didn't get any demerits for a dirty rifle, you got some for dropping it. You disengaged the bolt, hopefully without catching your thumb in the chamber, and clicked the trigger. Click. Just a small noise, amidst all the noises of inspection. Click. And you were done.

Why were the smallest guys always the cruelest captains? Zoo wondered if they issued short swords so that his captain wouldn't drag his. He smiled at this then realized that Cadet Captain Wakatsuki at four feet eleven was not smiling. He was saying, "Gimme ten, Mee-moto!" That little Napoleon couldn't say anything longer than three syllables. Zoo smiled again, grinned actually as he dropped to the ground. "That smile will cost you ten more, Mee-moto. And next time I wanna hear 'Yes, sir!' "

"Yes, sir," Zoo addressed the ground, nearly laughing out loud.

Lyle was getting the works. He was already giggling behind pursed lips, and his belly was jiggling. No matter how hard he tried, Lyle always looked disheveled in his uniform. He and Zoo had checked each other out before the parade in the locker room, but Lyle managed to scuff his shoes and tilt his cap to the back of his head and get his shirt and belt buckle and pants fly out of alignment and grow his hair just long enough to touch his ears. Lyle had even fainted once. He claimed that he had done it on purpose because he didn't want to stand in the sun, but he fell on his rifle and

bruised his cheek, which he then claimed was
gained in a fight with Sergeant Lima.

Zoo counted off twenty pushups.

Zoo was smeared with Vaseline all over his
upper body and face. His hair was tied back and
gathered in a hairnet and his ears were stuffed with
cotton. Someone cut a plastic straw in half and
stuck one up each nostril and applied more
Vaseline around his nose and eyes. The body cast
would take maybe twenty minutes and he'd be in
somebody's Masters of Fine Arts sculpture, but for
the moment, even before it happened, he felt the
ache again of having to be still, of being frozen in
one position. Already his breathing was shallow,
through his mouth.

"Don't move so much, I don't want to miss
your eyelids or else you'll lose all your eyelashes in
the plaster." Ordinarily he'd enjoy female hands
ministering to his face. There should have been
something sexual about so much Vaseline, but
there wasn't. The Vaseline felt thick and greasy and
heavy, like a blanket. No wonder channel-crossing
swimmers used it.

"Stop licking your lips, Kazuo, I'll have to
put some more on."

And it would be like the coma that he knew
would come eventually . . . a lifetime of waiting in
line to be judged, evaluated, cast. It made sense
that he'd have a long wait when he died too. He
certainly wouldn't go quickly. He smiled. Not
quickly but like now, waiting for the inevitable:
having to be silent and still, aching in the joints,
eyelids heavy, too heavy to lift, as if glued shut
with Vaseline, lips that were smeared with Vaseline

but seemed so dry he kept wanting to lick them.
He swallowed, that was all that was left for him to
do. He swallowed. At least there would be this
statue.

Everything in kung fu class started with the
horse position: fists cocked at the hips, left leg
lunging forward, right knee locked, foot angled.
This was culture in Chinese school. Zoo had the
choice of going to Japanese or Chinese language
school after his regular school days. He was both.
He chose Chinese school — despite the difficulty of
writing Kazuo in Chinese — because on Tuesdays
and Thursdays, the whole school studied Chinese
culture, kung fu or music. All the boys and most of
the girls chose kung fu leaving only the timid,
prissy girls to study moon harp.

For the kung fu students, the possibility of
learning to do the lion dance beat in their hearts.
The thundering drum and the tinny crash of the
cymbals sounded in their ears as two hundred arms
swept the air in the fast-slow rhythm of the first
set. When they were together, the only sounds
were the snap of their pant legs when they kicked
and the hissing, breathy exhale with the push and
pull of their hands. Everybody's halitosis is filling
the gym, Zoo thought. It's trapped in this hot,
closed place. The more Zoo watched the lion, the
more he truly believed it to have a life of its own.
Of course there were the advanced kung fu
students underneath the paper maché head and the
cloth body, but when it moved, it no longer
seemed that it was controlled. The good dancers
made it seem like an active, curious cat. At other
times it seemed like the cat was struggling to move

against the dancers . . . the dancers themselves,
head and rear, each wanting to go his own way.
The rear dancer just bent over and flapped the
sides of the beast, but the best of them made it
seem like it was breathing. Zoo thought of the lion
as he held the horse position, waiting once again
for the *see foo*, the teacher, to come and check him.
See Foo had started at the far end of the room and
faced each student squarely and pushed gently at
one shoulder or the other to see if your horse was
strong and steady. If you stumbled or fell you had
to do pushups. How the horse and all these
pushups would ever become the lion was beyond
Zoo. His knees ached and his front leg trembled
just as See Foo was two students away. One
student away, Zoo tried edging his back foot left
then right to see if he could stop his shaking leg.
He considered straightening up and dropping to
the floor in the pushup position and simply
listening for the number he had to do. See Foo was
right in front of him, holding the horse stance too,
simply looking into his eyes for a moment. He
corrected Zoo's back and pushed his stance lower,
said something in Chinese. Zoo's left knee seemed
to be waving wildly now and his teeth were
clenched. "Relax," See Foo told him. "Ee-see. Take
it ee-see. Balance . . . ready fo anybody from all
around. Breathe ee-see."

With that, See Foo swept past the rest of the
row in his baggy black trousers and instructed the
rows to form a circle around him and six of his
assistants. Each assistant held a weapon of some
kind: a large curved sword, a dagger with a tassel
on the handle, a long staff with a barb on the end,
a shorter wooden rod with a pitchfork on the end.

One assistant held two knives with wide curved blades, and one snapped a piece of rope between his hands. It was like watching the movies at the Golden Wall Theater. See Foo bowed to each in turn and they attacked one at a time. He dispensed with each quickly with a punch or a kick at half-speed or simply deflected them to the side. Then they came two at a time and three at a time, each time faster. The clang of the swords and the blades made the class wince and "oooh." See Foo became a flash of black trousers, the fabric cracking the air, snapping restlessly like the lion, always looking to the side and the rear. It ended with all six assistants disarmed, lying on the floor, and the entire class cheering See Foo. He bowed, smiling slightly to each of his assistants, then to the class.

He clapped his hands twice and said, "Positions." And the students were immediately back in their rows. "Horse position. Strong. Relax. Balance. Breathe in. Breathe out . . ." They breathed three times and with each exhale the excitement of the battle drifted toward the ceiling of the gym and whirled through the vents. Restless horses calmed.

When they placed the plaster over his eyes it seemed like it got noticeably darker through his closed eyes. They arranged his arms and their voices became muffled and indistinct when they covered his ears. Zoo wiggled his toes and shifted the position of his legs, the last remaining parts of his body that he could move. He rubbed the top of his left foot on the back of his right calf trying to get to an itch that started just as the first strip of plaster was laid on his body.

It would last him through the years: Zoo wouldn't even want to read about divers in iron lungs or people who spent time in oxygen chambers to preserve their youth or rebirthings floating in dark, salt water wombs or the tiny sleeping quarters for Japanese businessmen who had to work late.

As the plaster cast heated up, the stiffness in his joints became unbearable, like waiting for Sergeant Lima and Cadet Captain Wakatsuki to finish their inspection; like waiting for See Foo to correct his stance. And it would continue when his daughter, too, would feel the ache of waiting for Mrs. Kimura and Sensei to check, correct, inspect. When his sweat ran salty between his eyelids and stung and he was unable to wipe it away with the back of his hand; when his nose started to run and he could neither blow it nor suck it in or choke on it; when he felt the mucus creep down the back of his throat and when he tried clearing his throat, coughing it up with lips still closed. When the voices came back to him, "Een-spec-shun harms . . . don't move, don't move . . . the pushup position . . . *yut, gnee, sahn, see* . . . gimme ten, Mee-moto . . . count um off!" he pushed himself upright from the plywood sheet laid across two sawhorses. He clawed at his face and large pieces of plaster flaked off and the still wet parts clung in white smears across his cheeks. He grabbed a towel and wiped his face, muttered "Sorry, sorry," into it and walked out into the light. He blinked against the sun behind the overcast sky and stood picking at the cotton in his ears and listened for the drumbeat and the tinny clang of cymbals.

By the end of each class, everyone would be breathing hard and eyeing the clock for the last few minutes. The little girl no longer turned to check on her father as they all struggled to keep up with Sensei's cadence and the moves of two different karate sets, a complex series of punches, turns and kicks. They had to remember to "ki-ai" at the right moments. Even now, after weeks of practice there would still be a stray yell every now and then when someone forgot. When they did it right, the room moved in unison in a funny fast-slow rhythm that had by now become familiar. They would do it until Sensei was satisfied. They would be breathing heavily when Sensei stopped them and called them back to their positions. They straightened their gis, retied their belts, and faced Sensei in ragged rows, faces dripping and chests heaving. Zoo would like to be near the door where it was cooler. But the students standing at the end were expected to line up their rows. Zoo reluctantly followed the other row leaders in saying, "Line up!" as Sensei waited for each row to shuffle into place. Zoo would feel their eyes on him as he stood, feet apart, fists lightly clenched at his sides.

Sensei quietly commanded *"Ah-ji-me!"* and with his eyes closed counted off, *"Eesh, nee, san, shee. . . ."* Inhale. Exhale. Inhale. Exhale. They closed their eyes, grateful for the chance to cool down. It was near the end. At the beginning, Zoo could hear everyone's gasps for air wildly different from the count. By the fourth or fifth long exhale, the class would seem to breathe as one, the sweat would pour off their faces, the restless shuffling of feet would be quieted, and the husky gasps calmed.

TOADS

"So what you gonna be?" Barry went ask me.

"What *you* going be?" I went ask him back.

"I going be Zorro! Going be sharp man . . . my mahdah made me one cape and I going get one black hat and I went make one mask wit two eyeholes. I get one good stick fo use fo da sword. Going be sharp man. Shht, shht, shht!" Barry went make da Z fo Zorro wit his hand. Den he went poke me wit his finger, "En garde! So what you going be?"

"I donno yet, I told you. I just was going use my mask, da one we made in school."

"Eh, sick dat. J'like da pumpkin we had to make out of da paper bag. Sick."

Halloween time we always gotta do da same ting. We gotta bring one big paper bag and stuff um wit newspaper and tie da top wit string and paint um orange and da stem green and make one scary black face wit hammajang teet. Ho, hard fo carry dat ting home, da paint all flake off da package and da flakes go on your clothes and your mahdah put um out in da living room fo little while, even aftah Halloween pau.

"Why no be Hopalong Cassady. Or maybe da Long Ranger. Dah-dah dunt, dah-dah dunt, dah-dah dunt dunt dunt. . . ."

"Hiyo, Silvah! Awaaay. . . ."

"I thought you was going be Long Ranger. Dat would be sharp. Or what about da horse, Silva. Wynette Silva."

"Shaddap. I no like girls wit one moustache. Zorro going be good though."

"Yeah. What Jocks Full Loo going be?"

"Same. Everytime he like be one football player. And Na-na-nasubi said he like come wit us."

"What, dat tilly?"

Na-na-nasubi was kinda tilly so could make him scared kinda easy. He could play jacks good though, even bettah than da girls. Especially da one you gotta do around-da-worlds and no can show teeth. And he was smart. Everybody wanted to copy his homework paper so no good tease him too much, bumbye he no let you copy.

Barry said, "Before he come wit us, he gotta go trick o treat at da haunted house."

"Da green house?"

"Yeah."

"Ho, man!"

"If he like come wit us, he gotta go dere first and if he make it, den he can come wit us."

Had dis old green house on the way home from school, weeds all around, tall kine weeds and nobody next door cause was one Hawaiian Electric place with all the electric machinery and one wire fence all around and even had barbed wire on top. And on the other side of the haunted house was the dirt and gravel driveway wit the weeds so tall on the sides and in the middle only could walk where the tires went. And had toads all ovah in the grass, so even in the day, we only walked on the two dirt parts . . . even after the rain, when was muddy and had puddles, we walked only where the tires went cause once, we went walk little bit in the tall grass and the grass started moving and you could see um move because someting inside the tall grass went move and den stop and den move again. I went blast the place wit rocks and den all these toads started coming out of the grass. Hopping anykine way. J'like they was coming to get me. Ho, I went grab my school bag and make it! Barry said that his mother told him no touch toad bumbye you going get warts and anykine ooh-gee stuff. You going start to get bumps on top your skin and den your eyes going pop out, la dat. Bull liar I tink, yeah?

Spooky walk over dere, but me and Barry cut short by ovah dere everytime cause had one water pipe fo drink water and no mo old lady bother you about, "Get away from the water hose!" "Who told you you could use my water" and "You better close the pipe good, now."

The house was all green peeling paint and was all closed up. All the doors was closed, but some windows was broken and could see inside one room. Was only empty, all dusty and stink air.

One time Barry went take my coin purse, the plastic kine that look like one football and when you squeeze um, look like one mouth opening. No worry, nevah have any money dat time. He was fussing around wit um. You know, making like he was eating my hand, my ear, my nose, la dat. Den he went swing um around on da chain and he was making um go faster and faster and went fly off his hand and go ovah the electrical fence.

"Shet, I going had it," I told him. "I going get it, stupid. Now what I going do?"

Barry said, "No worry, I help you get um. I going get one stick and we can hook um and get um back." So we was trying to get the purse back from behind the fence and we was doing pretty good. I could just get my hand between the fence and the post and I was reaching wit all my might. I couldn't even turn my head fo see; my eyes was shut so I could reach as far as can. Barry was telling me go dis way or dat way, hold it, hold it. And den Barry nevah say nutting fo long time and I finally went turn and open my eyes and had one big Bufo wit his throat all puffed up right next to my face. Barry nevah say nutting, he was so scared of da toad. He jes was looking at da toad and da toad was looking at him, side-eye and was j'like he wanted fo get up and run away but he couldn't. I was scared too, but I wasn't as scared as Barry. I jes went tell, "Eh, nemmine da coin purse awready. We go."

I went tell Barry everytime I see one squashed toad on da road, dat it remind me of da Chinese herb man. I told him dat inside his shop get anykine dried up stuff . . . real animals, la dat. Jocks Full Loo said that probably even get some mummy heads and all shriveled up small pa-ke heads with eyeballs and nose hairs and bolo heads and warts and wrinkles and tough skin still yet warm, like one old wallet with some places worn smooth and some places all wrinkly. Barry nevah say too much about dat time and he jes went look at me like, "ooh-gee," when I told him about the Chinese man, so I nevah say nutting aftah dat.

The electricity place had anykine signs: WARNING, KEEP OUT, HIGH VOLTAGE, KEEP AWAY. SEVERE ELECTRICAL SHOCK HAZARD.

And always had one hum. Low hum. I liked dat place even though was little bit spooky wit all da signs la dat, but all da wires and the round tings wit da fins look like antennas to me. J'like Roy Rogers . . . I mean, Buck Rogers and da space ship and da alien guns. Once, I even saw one blue spark go "pak!" from one green antenna to da uddah one. And fo one second was all quiet. Nutting . . . no mo sound. Just da funny "tick" and "tack" of da metal. J'like was breathing, da machinery. Den went start up again. Spooky, da hum, da green machinery, da old green house, da green toads.

So had me and Barry, he was going be Zorro, and Jocks Full Loo, he was one football player. The helmet always so big dat Jocks Full had to walk around wit his head tilted back so dat he could see, uddahwise he gotta hold on to the face mask wit one hand and the football wit da uddah hand and den no mo hand fo hold his bag fo da candy. Sometimes he so stoopid sometimes. And Na-na-nasubi had one plastic suit wit one skeleton printed on top. His mahdah always buy him store-bought stuff. Barry went ask him, "Who you?" And Na-na-nasubi went say, "One sk . . . sk . . . skeleton." And Barry nevah catch and went tell, "You mean like Red Skeleton? He no look la dat. . . ." I had to laugh. Sometimes Barry smart. Sometimes he stupid. Sometimes no can tell.

Me, I was one shipwreck guy. Every year I one bust up shipwreck guy. My mahdah no buy me nutting; she no make me nutting. I gotta wear all da rag-bag stuff. I even rip um up so come more ugly and wind some old white rags around my head fo bandages and den get da Mercurochrome and make like get blood all on da bandages. Den I ask my bruddah use da matches and burn one old cork. . . . Daddy had da corks all in one old cookie can. You burn um until da stuff come all black and you can paint your face wit um. My bruddah can make um look j'like you all bus up but still yet alive from one explosion.

We was walking to da green house already. Me and Barry, den Jocks Full Loo little bit behind cause he was having hard time wit his helmet and his football and his trick o treat bag. I told you, eh. And had Na-na-nasubi mo behind den dat.

"So what, we going let Na-na-nasubi come wit us or what?" Barry went tell real loud so dat Na-na-nasubi could hear. "He no can come wit us if he going be one tilly. I no like no tillies come wit us. Tillies no can go da haunted house."

"Na . . . na . . . naht. I . . . I . . . I naht!" Na-na-nasubi went tell.

We told Na-na-nasubi that if he wanted to be on our gang, he had to go trick o treat at the haunted house wit us. He had to go and say, "trick o treat" and he couldn't just say, "chrickochreat" real fast and den run away. He had to say um slow and wait until somebody came to the door and no worry, we stay backing him up. But if one big toad went come to da door, he had to spit on um before he came back by us.

We went walk all da way to da haunted house, me and Barry and Jocks Full. Na-na-nasubi kept getting more and more behind. Could tell he was getting scared. Wasn't dat scary. Wasn't dark or anyting. We had to wait fo him by the porch of da house.

"Okay, go trick o treat at da door. You gotta stay dere by yourself now. And when somebody come to da door, den you call us," Barry told him.

Barry went give us da signal and we went make like we was backing him up and Barry went crawl undah da house right undah da porch. As soon as Na-na-nasubi went knock, Jocks Full and me went hide in the tall grass. Na-na-nasubi was getting kinda hard time even saying, "trick o treat."

"Tr . . . tr . . . tree . . ." And everytime he went knock on da door and say "trick o treat," Barry went bang one rock on da floor undah da house and make in one spooky voice, "Whaat? Whachulike? Who you?" Bang, bang, bang! And Na-na-nasubi went turn around and he nevah see us and da floor was going bang, bang, bang and we was hiding and laughing until I went tink of da toads dat must stay inside da grass and the Chinese medicine man wit da dried up animals and da dead toads on da street and da grass started moving and da electrical place came quiet. No mo hum, j'like the blue spark time. So I went get up from my hiding place and Na-na-nasubi went see me and started fo come by us. And den we went hear Barry say, "Shet. Shet. I went touch one toad!"

He came out from undah da house holding out his hand. "I thought da toad was da rock. Shet. Aw, shet. I going get all ugly."

We wanted to go by him fo see if he was going get all hairy or someting, but j'like we nevah like go by him jes in case he touch us.

"We go some houses," I said and jes started walking. Had me and Na-na-nasubi and Jocks Full in front and Barry was walking kinda behind us, crying little bit and everytime saying, "Shet." We had to wait fo him while he went back to his house and wash real good and change his Zorro costume cause he said might have toad shet on top.

"Whachumean might have toad shet! You ever seen toad shet before?" I told him. "We jes go already. You gotta be Zorro! Gotta go shht, shht, shht."

"Yeah but, must be toads shet," Barry went tell. "So wait fo me!"

"Okay, okay. But I nevah seen no toad shet."

We all wanted to be first to hit one house and ring da doorbell and say, "Trick o treat" cause you like, da kine, make da guys dat open da door scared, eh? And if get good stuff and plenny uddah guys at da door, you can get some candy den go to da back of da bunch and wait and den get somemore.

So when Na-na-nasubi was first, he went get kinda excited and scared. When he come la dat, he no can talk. Come stuck da words. He no can make um come out. "Trr . . . trrr . . . chrr . . . chrree . . . ah, shet!" Us guys we used to to it already. We no mind. Ass how he talk. You can feel um get stuck in his throat and j'like da words stay stuck in our throat too and we stay tinking: trick o treat, trick o treat, trick o treat. And everybody stay *tinking* um, but nobody stay saying um. And Na-na-nasubi stay all embarrassed and he just turn around to us and all of a sudden we all stay saying, "Trick o treat. Trick o treat. Trick o treat!" And Na-na-nasubi is saying um wit us . . . perfeck. He just needed to, j'like, warm up his voice; get um used to talking den it came out okay. Aftah dat he could say um

good, "Trick o treat! Trick o treat!" everytime.
     And aftah dat, we went call Barry
"Toadshet."

THE MOILIILI BAG MAN

One time by da Humane Society had one bummy guy at da drive-in. He was eating from da rubbish can. Yeah. My fren tell, "Ass da Moiliili Bag Man dat. Try look, get anykine plastic bag hanging from his belt. I tink he got um from Star Market."

Da Bag Man was looking through da rubbish can, eating da leftovers. Yeah, da throw way awready kind. Mostly he was looking fo da plate lunches, fo da extra rice. He no care, da guy. We was looking at him from our table and da girl behind da counter stay shaking her head watching da Bag Man. Little while more, da cook guy wit one dirty apron and one broom and dustpan came outside from da kitchen part fo sweep rubbish. Da cook guy was so stink, man, cause he jes go empty da dustpan, all dirt and rubbish la dat, right in da can dat da Bag Man was looking. Da Bag Man no say nutting . . . but da cook guy was stink, yeah? He could tell da Bag Man was still yet using da can.

Da Bag Man nevah know what fo do. He jes went stand dere by da can. Den he went check his bags: cigarette bag wit plenny butts and bus up kine cigarettes, someting else in one nudda one, and look like one half orange, peeled awready in one nudda one.

Russo, das my fren, told me dat people sometimes go give da Bag Man money jes so dat he go away from dem. Even if he not boddering dem, dey give um money. I guess dey no like look at him or someting. Funny yeah?

Anyway, I no can tell if da Bag Man is happy or sad or piss off or anyting l'dat cause he get one moosetash and skinny kine beard wit only little bit strands, stay hide his mout. But his eyes, da Bag Man's eyes, stay always busy . . . looking, looking, looking.

I look back at him, and to me, he ack like he little bit shame. We stay da only small kids sitting down at da tables, me and Russo, but da Bag Man ack like he no like know us.

Had one nudda guy in one tee-shirt was sitting at da table next to us was watching da Bag Man too. He was eating one plate lunch and afterwards, he went take his plate ovah to da Bag Man. Still had little bit everyting one top, even had bar-ba-que meat left.

"Brah," da guy tell, "you like help me finish? I stay full awready."

Da Bag Man no tell nutting, only nod his head and take da plate. I thought he would eat um real fast . . . gobble um up, you know. But was funny, he went put um down and go to da counter fo get one napkin and make um nice by his place . . . da fork on top da napkin. Even he took da plate out of da box, made um j'like one real restaurant. I wanted fo give him someting too, but I only had my cup wit little bit ice left. I awready went drink up all da Coke and was chewing da ice. Da Bag Man was looking at me now, not at me but at my cup. I nevah know what fo do cause j'like I selfish if I keep my cup but, nevah have nutting inside awready, so shame eh, if you give somebody someting but stay empty. But I nevah know what fo do cause I had to go awready. I thought I could jes leave da cup on da table or be like da tee-shirt guy and tell, "Brah, hea."

So I went get up and walk halfway and den turn back like I went foget throw away my cup. I went look at da Bag Man and say, "You like um?"

Da Bag Man nevah say nutting still yet, but I knew he wanted um so I jes went leave um on his table. I was curious fo see what he was going do wit um so I went make like I was fussing around wit someting on my bike. He went get out his hankachief from his front pants pocket and unwrap um. Had all his coins inside um and he went take out fifteen cents. Den he went take da cup to da window and point to da sign dat went say "Refills —15¢."

"Coke," he told da girl. Sly da guy! When I went pass him on my bike, I thought I saw him make one "shaka" sign to me. Wasn't up in da air, was down by his leg, j'like he was saying, "Tanks eh," to me.

Da next time I went see da Bag Man was by da shave ice place, Goodie Goodie Drive In. He was jes grinding one plate lunch, man. I donno if he went buy um. I doubt it, though. I thought I saw his busy eyes recanize me, but I donno. I jes went nod my head, jes in case he was telling "hi."

Aftah dat, j'like everyplace I go, he stay. Da Bag Man stay. One time me and my bruddah went Bellows Beach fo bodysurf and da Bag Man was dere. I heard my bruddah folks calling him Waimanalo Eddie but was him, da Moiliili Bag Man.

Was jes like I knew him by heart awready. I mean, j'like we was frens. I seen him by da Boy

Scout camp checking tings out. One ting about Boy Scouts, dey get plenny food, dey no run out, dem. But you know what, dey nevah know how fo cook rice. Dey went jam um up and had to dump um cause was too mooshy and wasn't right. Da Bag Man was right dere even befoa one scoop rice went inside da rubbish can. Could tell he was happy, boy. J'like he was dancing. His okole was wiggling and he was holding out his plastic bag for da throw way rice.

All da small kids, da Cub Scouts, started fo come around da Bag Man and ask him questions: "What you going do wit dat? How come you get so much tings in da bags?" One real small kid, wasn't even one Cub Scout went tell, "You one bum?"

Da Bag Man jes went smile and tell, "Dis fo my cat. He like dis kine rice." Den da Scout Mastah went try fo get all da kids fo go back by him. He went tell dem, "Come ovah hea. Da man jes going take da food fo his pigs or someting, *buta kaukau*. Come. I show you guys how fo make da fire so da ting no *pio*." But of course nobody was listening, dey still like hang around da Bag Man. Finally da Bag Man had to tell, "Eh, you fahdah stay calling you guys. Tanks, eh."

Aftah dat, I nevah see da Bag Man fo long time. I nevah see him, so I nevah even tink about him until one day, me and Russo went go Ala Moana beach and we went go fuss around by da end of da canal, by da pond part where sometimes get da guys wit da radio dat control da boats. Dose guys get piss off man, if you blast their boats wit rocks. Heh, heh, good fun though, sometimes.

But nevah have boats dis time so me and Russo was playing try-come, try-come. Ass when you try fo get da uddah guy come by you fo look at someting, but only stay bullshet like, "Try come, try come look dis doo-doo stay look like one hairy hot dog." And you try jazz um up so dat da uddah guy like come by you instead of him trying fo make you go by him.

So Russo went tell, "Try come, try come. Get one *ma-ke* man stay in da bushes. He stay *ma-ke* on anykine *food*, la dat!"

Shet. I knew no can be. Dat Russo, he such a bull-liar. So I was going tell him some interesting stuff about doo-doo but Russo went tell real scared, "Da *ma-ke* man leg went move!" So I went by him.

"He only sleeping, stupit," I went tell Russo real soft, jes in case da guy was really sleeping.

"No, he *ma-ke* die dead," Russo went say.

"How you know?"

"I know. Maybe somebody went murder him!"

By now Russo was making up anykine stories and talking mo loud and I knew wasn't *ma-ke* man cause da legs was moving somemore and could hear somebody talking from inside da bushes.

"Sucka. Sucking kids, beat it befoa I smash your face."

Was da Bag Man. He was blinking his eyes real plenny and den he went look at us, stink eye. Russo was getting chicken and was backing up little by little, but I jes went stay.

We jes went look at each uddah, but dis time da Bag Man's eyes wasn't so busy. He jes started fo rip up one coconut leaf. Was sharp, man. He had one supah long fingernail on his thumb dat was jes right fo rip da coconut leaf into skinny strips yeah, and little while mo he went make one bird out of

75

da coconut leaf. He nevah say nutting. He jes went stick um behind his ear. He went look at me, den at Russo, den at me again. I thought he was going scold us or someting, but he jes went start making one nudda bird. Only dis time he nevah go so fast. In fack, he went real slow, j'like he was teaching me how. When he was pau, he went give um to me and den he jes went split, even befoa I went tell um tanks.

When I went home, I went put da Bag Man's bird on top my bureau and even if I nevah see him long time aftah dat Ala Moana park time, I went tink of him everytime I saw da bird dere on top da bureau. Sometimes I try practice make birds, but I couldn't do um like da Bag Man. I could almost do um, but mines came out funny kine. I used to wonder if da Bag Man was in Waimanalo or if he was grinding food at da drive-in or if he was making birds too at Ala Moana.

And den one day I was fussing around wit his bird, was all brown and coming had-it. Nevah have nutting fo do, so I went try make da bird again. I kept looking at da Bag Man's bird and den back at mines one. Back and fort. Back and fort. I had to laugh cause must've been funny. Must've looked like da Bag Man's busy eyes . . . looking, looking, looking.

Den shet, was so easy. I went make um! Came out perfeck! I went make my bird look exact like his one. I went get somemore coconut leaf and try one mo time cause even I nevah believe. Da stuff came out again!

I wanted fo go Waimanalo or Ala Moana or drive-in right away . . . but I nevah see him aftah dat time at Ala Moana park. And everyplace I go, I stay looking, looking, looking. But if I was to see him, I would make one bird fo him and den hold my hand down wit da shaka sign and make, "Tanks, eh."

ON MY HONOR

On my honor, I will do my best,
To do my duty to God and my country,
And to obey the Scout Law.
To help other people at all times,
To keep myself physically strong,
Mentally awake, and morally straight.

A scout is cheerful:

"You sure you no like go Cub Scouts? I gotta take Henry to his meeting and Mama going beauty shop," Daddy went ask me.

"I no like go, I told you. No ways I going Cub Scout. I going be da oldest kid there. Cub Scout too baby!"

"Well, no ways he going come Boy Scout meeting wit me. He too baby!" Henry went say.

"I no like go wit you anyway, stupid!"

"Okay, okay," Daddy went tell. "You jes stay home by yourself den. No let anybody come in da house. You can go play wit Brynie next door when he come home."

"I no like play wit Brynie."

"How come you no play wit Brynie nowadays?" Daddy went tell.

"Cause he one punk."

"Cause he no like play wit you, stupit," Henry went razz me.

"Okay. That's enough." Daddy said. "Uncle's phone numbah in da book. Call him if get emergency. Maybe tonight we can go see Christmas lights or someting."

"Shoot, yeah!"

When Daddy take Henry to Boy Scout meeting on Saturdays, I no like go wit dem awready. He still yet ask me if I like join Cub Scout, but I no like go awready. Junk.

A scout is obedient:

Da first time Daddy went ask me if I wanted fo join Cub Scout was when Henry went from Cub Scout to Boy Scout. He had one new uniform: khaki shirt, khaki pants, belt, hat. Henry so slow wit tings. Everyting he put on had to be jes right. And Henry, he tink I his slave or someting. He tell me, "Go get my hat. Go get my shoes. Go get my belt. And no touch da buckle with your fingers now. If you touch um, you going make um funny kine. I no like you get your fingerprints on um." And all kine other stuff la dat.

Perfeck had to be. When he finally pau put da hankachief around his neck, he went look sharp, man. I almost nevah recanize him. J'like he came mo tall and when he practice salute in front da mirror, was j'like Army.

Daddy came by us and went tell, "You ready? Hurry up!" Daddy was wearing his new uniform too. He was going be da Scout Mastah.

I went tell, "You guys look j'like Army, Daddy."

He told me, "Oh yeah? You like join too? You can join Cub Scout if you like. You old enough now. Going get new kids join next week. If you be good, you can join. You gotta take care your uniform and do all your homework, though."

"Yeah, I going be be good, Daddy. I like wear uniform. Den all us guys can be Army."

"Scouts, Hiram. Scouts."

A scout is loyal:

I was good da whole week. I even went foget to call Brynie one punk in school. When Henry wasn't home, I went try find his Cub Scout uniform. He nevah hang um up aftah he got his new Boy Scout one, so was all had-it on da floor in his closet. But I found his cap, blue wit yellow lines and da bear patch in front. Ass means, Cub Scout. When you Cub Scout, you gotta salute wit two fingahs, you know. I went practice. When I get my uniform, I going take care of um, not like Henry.

I went look at Henry's Boy Scout buckle. He put Brasso on top and polish um until come perfeck. J'like one mirror. Even aftah stay perfeck, he always stay breathing on um and polishing um somemore. J'like one golden mirror, da buckle. Your face come fat when you look close at um and come foggy and den come clear and den come foggy again.

When Cub Scout day came, I went ask Daddy where my uniform. He told me jes wear Henry's old one.

"Ho man, Henry's one junk. I no like wear his one. Everytime I gotta wear his stuff."

Henry went say, "Not junk!"

"No lie! Stay all jam up in your closet!"

"You went look in my closet? I told you, you no can go in dere unless I say you can! Daddy, Hiram went inside my closet witout asking!"

Daddy finally went tell, "Eh, quiet you two. Hiram, you wear Henry's one or else you no wear nutting and you no go!"

"Okay den," I went tell, but I was tinking dat Henry was still one punk and his uniform was still yet junk.

Daddy said Mama could hem up da pants and fix um so dat no can tell was Henry's. He told me he was going wear his old blue Cub Scout leader one too, so dat us two could match-match. Mama said da uniform was still yet good, only needed to fix up little bit. Mama was jes telling me fo turn la dis and la dat and she sew little bit and pretty soon went fit okay. She told me she was going buy me one new hankachief, I mean neckachief slide. One gold one, because Henry's one da gold went all come off. Henry lucky I nevah tell her was bus up because he went file um down one time fo see if was gold all da way through.

Henry was acking wise, making like, "Ha-huh, you gotta wear my old uniform. . . ." Den he started fo say, "Eh, Ma! He no can go meeting wit my badges! You gotta take um off! Right, Daddy? He gotta start from da beginning, no can cheat! And he gotta learn da Cub Scout Promise!"

"Shaddup! I not one cheatah!"

Mama nevah say nutting but she went make da noise in her throat, "Ahhgh huh." Den she went say soft, "So much humbuck."

Daddy was waiting and getting mad cause he started fo shake his keys in his pocket. Henry only was saying, "Ass mines! Ass mines! Da badges stay mines!"

Daddy jes went take da scissors and went cut da threads holding on da patches. He cut halfway on each one and den went rip da rest. Almost went pull my shirt down, he pull so hard.

"Here!" He went give da patches to Henry. "You satisfy now?"

I went look my uniform in da mirror and now had anykine dark blue spots all ovah where da patches was.

"You punk Henry! You punk! I no like go! I no like go awready!"

So I no like go Cub Scout anymore. I rather stay home. I would've been one good Cub Scout though:

> I, Hiram Wong, promise to do my best,
> to do my duty to God and my country,
> to help other people at all times and
> to obey the Law of the Pack.

A scout is trustworthy:

When da car went down da driveway, I went put on da Christmas tree lights, even if was daytime. I started fo shake da presents. Sounded like all was clothes so far except fo someting small and heavy from Aunty Irene and someting like one game from Aunty Nellie. Da game one I could move da ribbon to da side and peel off da tape at da end fo see what was. Parcheesi. Not bad. Now I no need ask Henry fo use his one. He so stink sometimes. I gotta do anykine stuff fo him befoa he lend me his game. And den he no even play wit me. I gotta play two colors by myself. Da uddah box I couldn't tell what was cause I couldn't move da ribbon. Wide kine ribbon. Liberty House box. Aunty Irene always give good stuff.

Da lights was warming up and da bubble ones started fo make bubbles. Sharp when da bubbles start to go. I tink supposed to look like candles but it jes tubes of color water. And when it warm up it start to make bubbles, j'like aquarium bubbles, from da bottom of da lightbulb. If you squint at da Christmas lights, come almost like colored stars. J'like night time.

I went to Daddy's room and went check around his loose change ashtray. Once I went find thirty-five cents dat went fall undahneat da bureau so I went keep um. I needed money fo buy cigarettes eh? I no tink he went miss um. I figgah he donno about da money dat went fall out of his loose change ashtray. Ass like finding money in da street almost, yeah?

If you smoke one cigarette and look at da Christmas lights, da lights come hazy through da smoke. J'like stay coming cold and da smoke is da kine you make when you breathe in da cold air.

My favorite ornament is da silvah one with da picture of one small house with sparkly snow all around and on da roof get one chimney wit sparkly smoke coming out. Can see da bubble lights in da shiny parts. J'like fo real. J'like da sky stay moving.

A scout is friendly:
I could hear Brynie fooling around outside. He probably was going smoke in da back of da garage. Brynie live next door to us. He bad sometimes. One time when I was small, walking home from school, he went come by me on his bike and tell me, "You like me pack you on my bike? I ride you home."

"Sure."

"Okay. You jes gotta go buy me cigarettes from da machine at Puunui Store. I give you da money."

"Shaddup. I no can buy cigarettes, da lady going scold me."

"No worry. You jes buy um while I stay looking inside da store so da lady no see you. I buy you kakimochi. What kine you like?"

"Da kine wit da seaweed on top. Da nori."

"Okay den, here da money. Buy Kools and no foget da matches."

"You sure da lady not going nab me?"

"Yeah, yeah. No be chicken. You jes wait until I buy da kakimochi and she go in da back to da cash register. When she make da cash register "chee-ching" la dat, you put da money inside da cigarette machine and get da cigarettes. Kools, now."

"Make sure you buy da kakimochi wit nori. . . ."

"You ready? Get ready now."

". . . and plenny shoyu on top."

A scout is helpful:

Brynie went inside da store and told da lady he wanted five cents worth kakimochi. I went hang around by da cigarette machine.

I went by Brynie to see if da lady was putting da right kine kakimochi. I was watching her scoop from da big glass kakimochi jar and she was missing all da good ones . . . da ones wit plenny nori an da real brown kine wit plenny shoyu. I was tinking dat if I could scoop kakimochi, I wouldn't scoop any broken kine or junk kine. Every one would have one big black square of nori and every one would be shiny wit plenny shoyu.

"Get good kine!" I went whispah to Brynie. Brynie was waving at me to go get ready by da cigarette machine, but I had to make sure I got da good kine kakimochi.

"Go! Go awready!" Brynie went tell me kinda loud and da lady went look at me and den at Brynie.

I went by da machine and put da coins inside right when da lady went open da cash register.

"Chee-ching!"

Was loud, man, when da coins went inside da machine. I went look around fo see if anybody was watching me. Nevah have nobody. I went press "Kools" and "Matches" and I was going make-it awready when I decided fo try out da coin return button too, jes in case was going get any money coming back. Jes when I went press da coin return button, I heard da lady yell at me, "Eh boy, you no can buy cigarettes. You too young. Wassamattah you!" Nabbed! She going tell my mahdah. Brynie not going buy me kakimochi. I going had-it!

"You da Wong boy, eh? Wait till I tell your mahdah."

Brynie went wave at me, "Go! Go!" I went grab da cigarettes and run home.

Punk Brynie! Punk! He made me do um!

A scout is brave:

Mama was talking on da telephone when I got home. I was hoping dat da store lady nevah call her. She was talking Chinese, so I tink she was talking to my grandma, Ah Po. I couldn't tell if she was talking about me. I went try listen fo my Chinese name, but she was talking too fast. I couldn't tell if dey was talking about me or cigarettes. I went hide da cigarettes in my closet. I went hide in there too, fo little while until she went hang up. Punk Brynie, if da lady call up my mahdah, I going tell was him da one dat went make me buy da cigarettes.

I could hear him next door yelling fo me fo come out, "Hiram! Hiram! You owe me someting! Hiram! Where my stuff?" He was so piss off dat he started fo throw Kleenex at our house. Real punk, yeah? He go wet um first in one bucket and when stay all wet, he take da ball of Kleenex and throw um at our house so da stuff stuck to da wall. Pwop . . . pwop . . . pwop. He nevah know my mahdah was home and she went tell Brynie she was going call da cops. He such a punk he went tell her, "Go. See if I care." Pwop. Pwop.

My mahdah came mad, boy. She went tell, "I going tell your fahdah when he get home. I going call da policeman right now." And she started fo dial da phone. *Den* Brynie came scared.

My mahdah was telling real loud, so he could hear, "I going call dem. I calling da policeman right now!" Brynie went run inside his house and could hear him crying. Little mo I was going tell her was my fault cause I had Brynie's cigarettes, but he da one dat went force me fo buy um and da lady at da store went nab me, so I went run away and *please* no send Brynie jail. My mahdah started fo talk Chinese in one mad voice. Ho. She only went call Ah Po.

By da time Daddy came home, da lady still yet nevah call. I had to run answer da telephone everytime, but everytime wasn't her. Daddy nevah say nutting either, so I figgah I was safe. Couldn't tell though. Fo long time I went walk home across da street from da store and had to go real fast jes in case da lady was looking out fo me. And punk Brynie nevah gimme da kakimochi, so I nevah give him his cigarettes. Good fo him.

A scout is clean:

"I like drag. Drag. Gimme drag." Ass how all da guys talk when dey like smoke. I used to wondah how dey can talk when dey get da cigarette in their mout.

When you smoke, if you squint your eyes little bit, you look tough, man. I went try look da mirror and practice holding da cigarette la dat. I no really smoke. I jes puff. You get cancer if you take um in your lungs like Brynie. Brynie, he smoke up, him. He take um in and blow smoke rings. But I no need take um in my lungs fo blow smoke rings. I can jes puff and make smoke rings. Sharp dat, smoke rings. You watch um until dey disappear into da air. Sometimes j'like you can see um fo long time even aftah nobody else can see um. If you was watching um fo long time, you know where da ting stay. And even aftah you no can see um, you know it stay dere. Try watch.

Sharp da Christmas lights when you smoke and squint your eyes. Da smoke rings was making um little bit fuzzy and you jes watch da bubbles go.

Little while mo, I had to clean up befoa Daddy dem came home: hide da cigarettes, throw way da ashes in da dirt by da garden, throw da butt ovah da fence, and turn on da fan fo blow da smoke out of da house.

When Daddy dem came home, he went ask me, "What you went do?"

"Nutting."

Henry went check da Christmas tree, "Anybody went bring new presents?"

"Nutting fo you."

"Eh, you went burn da lights eh? Daddy, Hiram went burn da lights. You said couldn't burn da Christmas lights daytime. Try look, still yet hot! You said burn too much electricity!"

I jes went ask Daddy, "We can go see Christmas lights tonight?"

Daddy said, "I guess so, since you went stay home by yourself today. We can go see da Portagee's lights."

A scout is thrifty:

Christmas time get plenny guys put up lights by our house. My fahdah no like put up lights. "Waste electricity. Burn too much," he always tell. But he *like* go see somebody else's lights. We always wait until he tell, "We go see da Portagee's Christmas lights." Dat means we going riding around night time fo see da lights. Anybody's lights. But to Daddy, if dey put up lights, dey must be Portagee.

Every year we go see da house by Houghtailing Street. Daddy get lost everytime. He gotta drive around little while befoa he can figure out how fo get there. But when he turn da las corner, you know he get um when you can see da rocket ship, all small kine light bulbs, taking off from da garage roof, shooting fo da moon, outlined in red and green bulbs and blinking off and den on.

And when you come close, ho, da buggah is sharp. Da whole house is light bulbs. Outline everyting: da roof, da windows, da steps, da railing, anykine man. In da front get, da kine, da Tree Wise Men and Mary and Joseph and da animals and Jesus la dat. Da trees in da yard all get lights, but da bes is da Santa Claus on da rocket ship sled . . . all outline in light bulbs.

Everybody come fo see dat house. Sometimes little mo get accidents when da drivers stay looking at da stuffs and their car still yet moving. Almost bang da parked cars cause only get nuff room fo one car fo go. Mama everytime gotta tell Daddy fo watch out fo da cars while Daddy stay hanging out da window saying, "Summagun, must burn plenny electricity."

I wish we could put up lights in our yard. But Daddy, he no like. Burn too much electricity. Even Halloween time he no like leave da porch light on cause burn too much electricity. But I figgah he jes no like da kids come trick o' treat our house. Still yet I go tell, "Ho, I wish we could have lights la dat in our yard."

Mama only make da noise in her throat, "Ahhhgh . . . huh," but she no say nutting. Ass means "no" when nobody answer and Mama make da noise.

Daddy had to park da car cause had traffic jam. I saw some guys going inside da house. I went ask Daddy, "We can go inside da house too?"

"Nah, no can."

"Can. Try look, dey going!"

"Go if you like den," he went tell me.

I was scared fo go myself, so Daddy told
Henry fo go wit me. I tink Henry wanted fo go too,
but he always gotta make like, "Wow, man. I gotta
take *him*." But dis time he only went say, "Ho man,
why me everytime."

"Go awready, or no go," Daddy went scold
us.

So we went.

A scout is reverent:
I was scared of da Portagee lady by da door.
She was fat and her okole was holding back da
porch screen door. She had light purple glasses
hanging around her neck from da eyeglass string
stuff, j'like da school librarian. And she had
freckles by her chi-chi's.

Inside da house was j'like Michael Costa's
house. Everyting stay on top one doily: anykine toy
animals, cats and lions and tigers, da kine you win
at carnaval; had pictures, anykine pictures,
graduation pictures wit da feather lei hanging on
top da frame, had one of one kid in one Boy Scout
uniform and had one Scout sash hanging on da
wall wit plenny merit badges. Almost no mo room
on da sash awready, had so much badges. And had
Christmas lights all over inside da house too. And
had Christmas trees made out of anykine stuff:
telephone book Christmas tree, wire hanger
Christmas tree, Kleenex Christmas tree, toothpick
Christmas tree, even pop-top from da soda can
Christmas tree.

Had to jes follow da line around da room fo
see all da lights and da different kine trees. Some
was on top one motor and was turning around. In
da back had one Jesus statue and one wishing well.

Everybody was throwing money inside um. Fo good luck, I guess. Had one Portagee man, da fahdah I tink, was by da wishing well part. I figgah he had to watch da money. He was watching me too, maybe fo see if I was going give anyting or maybe fo make sure I wasn't going swipe nutting. He nevah look at Henry la dat. He jes gimme da stink eye and smoke his cigarette. I donno why he was looking at me, I nevah do nutting. I heard people throwing da coins. Plop . . . plop . . . plop.

Somebody went drop one coin on da floor and it went roll undahneat da wishing well. I went bend down fo see where went. And next time when I went look up, was j'like da man stay laughing at me. He went blow one smoke ring and it went float past me, round and wiggily. And I went look at da plastic Jesus all lighted up and da wishing well and all da coins in da water and all da Christmas trees coming hazy from da smoke, and I wanted fo go home awready.

I told Henry, "C'mon we go awready."

"Not yet, we gotta follow dis line. Get some more stuff fo see."

"Ass okay, we jes go in front. Can cut. Da ladies ovah there taking too long time." I couldn't wait.

A scout is courteous:
I jes went by da door awready and left Henry in da line. I was trying fo find my slippahs on da porch and da big Portagee lady went gimme one candy cane.

"Tank you," I told her. She nevah say nutting back. She went put on her glasses and went look at me j'like she was memorizing my looks and my clothes and she went lean ovah da railing fo see which car I was going back to. On da way out, could see all da back of all da lights, da back of da rocket ship and da Santa Claus and da moon. Had anykine wires all ovah da place and had scrap wood was holding up da Tree Wise Men and da back of da animals was all bus up, crack and patch up wit masking tape. Everyting look kinda had-it.

Henry came down da steps aftahwards and went tell me, "Stupit, what you went do? Da lady was giving you stink eye. She nevah even gimme candy cane she was so busy watching you!"

"Nutting. I nevah do nutting!"

Daddy was still hanging out da window when we went back to da car.

"Terrific, eh?" he went tell us.

"Not bad," Henry went say.

I jes went say, "Burn too much, Daddy. Burn too much."

A scout is kind.

J'LIKE TEN THOUSAND

My fahdah stay so tight, so pa-ke. He no like buy firecracker, man. He only buy one five hundred pack fo burn at New Year's time. Ho man, everybody get da thousands or da five thousand strings or even da ten thousand strings but Daddy, he no like buy nutting fo me. He only say, "Jes throw away money dat. One boom and pau. All dat money go up in smoke. And da ting only make rubbish." He so tight. Every year, he buy only one five hundred pack fo burn, fo good luck. And he only buy me stuff like cracker balls or sparkalahs. And I only get one hundred pack sometimes or sometimes one pack of baby Camels, ass da real small firecrackers dat only make one soft pop, from Firecracker Uncle. Good ting I get Firecracker Uncle or I wouldn't get nutting fo burn.

Firecracker Uncle always get one Christmas party his house every year on da night befoa Christmas. His Christmas party da bes man, cause everytime he give firecracker to da kids. Kids not supposed to pop firecracker, but he give us. He da Firecracker Uncle.

Everybody gotta eat dinner first. But everybody know what going get aftahwards, so dey eat real fast and try figgah out where Firecracker Uncle going sit. Da small kids donno what going happen, so easy fo get dem fo move from da good spots. Jes gotta tell, "Eh, dis my spot. You gotta

99

move. Try look, you see dis mark on da floor, ass means dis my spot!"

When Auntie Sadie pass out da song sheets aftah everybody pau eat dat means pretty soon Firecracker Uncle going come. Of course everybody know we gotta sing da "Twelve Days of Christmas" Hawaiian style and Uncle Boo-boo everytime wave his beer when come to "ten can of bee-ya." And den we gotta sing "Jingle Bells" and right in da middle get Firecracker Uncle, I mean Santa Claus, ringing da doorbell. Auntie Sadie send da smallest kid fo go open da door. She throw da ack, she tell, "I wondah who dat?" Anyway, it only Firecracker Uncle. Can tell cause when he give out da presents, Auntie gotta bring his glasses udderwise he no can read da tags. And Firecracker Uncle get gold teet and his hands always smell like fish from selling fish at da fish market, so gotta be him, yeah? He give out all da presents calling out our name one by one. Da small kids little bit scared but us big guys not scared. Jes gotta go, shake hands l'dat and he give you your present.

Dis da only Christmas present dat my mahdah let me open befoa Christmas cause everybody else's mahdah let da kids open. Dis time, inside da big kids present had one pack firecrackers, numbah one hundred kine, one pack sparkalahs, and one pack cracker balls.

Was funny cause aftah all da kids went open their presents, my mahdah and everybody's mahdah made all da kids go to uncle and tell him in Chinese, *"Dough jay, Goo Geong."* You know, fo say tank you to uncle. Was funny cause everybody went line up and say, "Tank you, Uncle" when he still yet was in his Santa Claus suit. Anyway, every year da big kids got firecracker from Firecracker Uncle. Of course da small kids only got sparkalahs and cracker balls. But if Uncle gave you firecrackers, ass means you was old enough fo burn.

Aftah all dis was pau, we had to sing "Jingle Bells" again and when Firecracker Uncle came back in his regular clothes, he went try ack like wasn't him. But was, yeah?

When we went home, I wanted to open up my firecracker package, but my mahdah said I couldn't touch um until New Year's Eve.

Ho man, sometimes I stay tink about um though. I tink, how many get inside? I wondah if every one going pop. I start figgah-ing out where in da yard I going pop um. Like by da mock orange hedge, where if you put one inside da middle, all da leaves fall down when you blass um. By da rock wall by where da toad live. By da witch lady's house. You gotta have all da spots ready you know, cause no mo dat much inside da pack, no can waste um. Ass why you gotta open up da pack of firecrackers and unwind da string dat hold da pack together so dat you can burn um one by one. I jes wish sometimes I could have one pack dat I could jes burn all one time. One ten thousand string, maybe.

New Year's Eve aftah I pau eat dinner, my mahdah finally went tell I could go pop my firecrackers. You know, if you count da one hundred pack, no mo one hundred firecrackers inside, only get thirty seven. Ho, da gyp! My fahdah said dat da hundred pack supposed to mean dat it *sound* like one hundred explosions not dat it get one hundred firecrackers inside. I nevah believe. I jes told him, "I wish I had one ten thousand one. Would be sharp yeah? One long string, all popping wit sparks and fire all ovah. . . ." My fahdah nevah say nutting. He was jes going be tight.

So aftah I went blass all of mines, I went go see if Brynie next door had anymoa. Sometimes he gimme some. Brynie's fahdah always buy him plenny packs. By da time we was pau wit our firecrackers and we went play cracker ball fight wit slingshot, Brynie's fahdah was ready fo pop his long strings. My fahdah came out of da house and even if he went say to Mama, "Mistah Kawamura going burn money again!" he came out fo watch too. Sometimes Mistah Kawamura get five, mebbe six strings. Five thousands and one supah-long ten thousand fo da end. My fahdah, he no like buy but he like watch um pop. I tink he like some of da good luck come by him. Mistah Kawamura got out da laddah and went hang up da strings from da basketball net. He make us laugh, Mistah Kawamura, cause he always get one cigarette in his mout while he stay hanging up da firecrackers. Everytime his cigarette come close to da firecrackers, me and Brynie, we jump back, man. Den when everyting ready, he check to make sure me and Brynie stay on da porch and he wave to my Daddy and he take da cigarette out of his mout and light um. He jest light um and den run away fast. He came by us fo watch.

I like da bomb part da bes. Das da las part of da string when get plenny firecrackers pop all at da same time. When Mistah Kawamura say we can, me and Brynie go look fo da ones dat nevah pop and save um so dat we can pop um bumbye.

Pretty soon only get smoke. Only can see Mistah Kawamura running through da smoke fo hang up one nudda string. Only can see his cigarette come bright jes befoa he light da string. Den only can see him running out from da smoke and den da bomb at da end. PRAAAWK! I foget awready how many strings he went pop dis time but was real plenny. I jes knew was pau when he went pop da ten thousand one.

Mama went tell Daddy dat midnight went pass already. Mama went light da punk fo burn our firecrackers and Daddy went get his five hundred pack. First, he practice swing his hand couple times, fo practice where he going throw um. No can hang up da five hundred pack, too small dat. Daddy jes throw um. He went rip open da bottom jes little bit and pull out da fuses.

"Mama," he went wave his hand fo da punk and Mama gave him da punk and he went practice throw somemoa times. Me and Mama stay little bit back, kinda scary when Daddy getting ready fo throw. Daddy, he always light um and den he wait little bit, he no throw um right away. He wait until da ting is lighted good. Daddy went light um and den he went wait little bit. Me and Mama went move little mo back. Da stuff was spitting sparks and fire befoa he finally went throw um. And when he went throw um, was j'like one rocket. Da fuses was spitting sparkles and den while still yet was in da air, da firecrackers start fo pop. POP . . . POP . . . POP. Slow and den got faster. POP, POP, POP, POP. And den jes when hit da ground: PROPP, POP, POP. PRAAWK! Not too long da pops but was sharp still yet.

Den Daddy went signal Mama and tell, "Get
da uddah one, Mama." And Mama got one nuddah
pack from inside da house. I thought only had one
pack, but Daddy had one nudda one. He went look
at me and tell me, "You like pop um?"

I wasn't too sure, but he jes went tell me,
"Heah, come o'heah.' And he went gimme da
firecrackers. Den he went show me how you can
tell which side fo open, da side dat get da fuses.
Den he hold my hand and we went practice throw.

"Swing la dis," he went tell me and he swing
his hand holding my hand and I can see da
firecracker pack flying awready wit da sparks and
da fire shooting from da fuse part. Like one rocket.

"You going help me eh, Daddy?" I went ask
him.

"No worry. No worry." And we went
practice again. And again. And den he went say,
"We ready, Mama." Mama went gimme da punk.
And Daddy and me went line up: me in front,
Daddy in back. His hands was big on top mines;
punk hand and firecracker hand.

"You ready?" I only stay looking down at da
punk and da five hundred pack and Daddy's hand
went put da punk by da firecracker fuse. I wanted
fo throw awready, but Daddy's hand was holding
me back. I like throw, I like throw! And den I went
jes look at da fuse and da punk and was jes
starting fo light. Jes little bit. And was j'like I went
throw um already I could see da sparks and da fire
and da pops in da air.

And den it went catch good. Was spitting
sparks anykine way. And my hand wasn't fighting
Daddy's anymoa and we went throw da
firecrackers da same way we went practice and da

stuff was spitting sparks and fire in da air. Like one rocket. And while was still in da air, it started fo pop: POP, POP, POP, PRAAWK! Daddy's hand went let go mines.

Was only five hundred, but Daddy and me, we went pop um j'like was ten thousand.

NO MISTAKING

"Dis morning, ho, erryting buckaloose. I thought I was gone wit da wind. Dey come massage me. Ho, da rough dey rub me. I donno how come dey so rough. And all kine doctors stand around my bed. Four doctors one time. My doctor ask me, 'Mr. Lee, you know who I am?'

"I tell, 'Of course. You my doctor. And dat my sister Florence and my brother-in-law Ed, and my brother Howard and Irene.' Get four doctors checking up on me and da man nurse rubbing me and massaging me rough. I donno why dey so rough. Dey push me all over.

"Chee, dey went call everybody to da hospital like dat, just like when my mother died. Chee . . . maybe I was little mo gone wit da wind, yeah? Otherwise dey no call up everybody like dat, yeah?

"Chee, maybe little mo gone wit da wind," he circled his hand in the air. I imagined the wind.

"But now I feel okay. But dis morning, gone with da wind. Huh, da Buddha, Kwan Yin, look aftah me. No come fo me yet.

"Thirty-five years I live by myself. Take care myself . . ." he trailed off and looked out the window. The view outside the hospital room was of exhaust pipes from the kitchen and the boiler room and across the way, windowless concrete walls. "But me," he continued, "I have self control

. . . no have temptation."

"Plenty ladies like marry me, you know. Dey pinch my ear, pinch my cheek, pinch down there," he pointed toward his groin and grinned.

"But I no damn fool. If I marry now, I gotta give half da house to her. What fo, when I got em so dat da two girls, my two granddaughters, get da house when I die? I no need wife. Night time, I get lonely, I hug my blanket, hug my pillow, dat's all.

"Me, I like girls, you know. Boys, you tell dem someting dey say 'Yeah, yeah,' but in their mind, dey fight you.

"Well, I'm eighty-eight years old. At least I got to see my granddaughter get married. Japanee boy. Well, dat's okay you know. I took care of dem when dey were babies, you know. Later on they can have dis house. Good girls. Good to have girls.

"I think dis American food they give me better fo me, you know. One scoop rice only, little bit meat, vegetables. Me I like eat *hahm gnee,* salt fish, you know. Ho, dat buggah make you eat rice. . . .

"Now no mo *hahm gnee,* no mo *hau see,* oysters, yeah. Heh, I used to steam da *hau see* and eat wit rice. Put oyster sauce, *hau yau,* on top. Ho, da good dat. No good eat dat kine, too salty, bad for da high blood pressure, but I like eat dat, boy. Da social worker like me go inside one of dose homes, but I no can eat dat kine Filipino food. You know da Filipinos run da nursing homes nowdays . . . ho, I no can eat dat kine. I tell her, 'Yeah, yeah,' but I thinking, 'I not going to dat kine place, eat Filipino food.' They no can make me go dat kine place, yeah?

"Waste time sit around here. I told my doctor, 'What fo I stay in here only sit around. I can sit around at home. Same ting!' I went call up my sister Florence dis morning, tell her to bring my clothes and my wallet. Mo bettah I catch da cab go home! She told me I no can go until da doctor say I can go home. 'He said pretty soon,' I told her. Pretty soon."

At home, Uncle Kam Chong looked even thinner than when he was in the hospital. Pale and thin, just flesh hanging on a skeleton after almost being "gone with the wind." He had always been skinny. But now he was so thin, I couldn't imagine him anymore with one of those white paper caps serving up sodas and malts behind the fountain at Benson-Smith Drugstore downtown. It was one of those fountains with the tall swivel stools and the chrome gooseneck spigots: water, soda water, and Coke. I remembered barely being able to see over the counter waiting for my Coke float with an extra cherry and watching Uncle's ears. He had interesting ears, just right it seemed for holding up the paper cap, and long floppy lobes which years later explained the funny kinship I had always felt between my uncle and the Kwan Yin statue at the Academy of Arts. There always was a peaceful comfortableness about being around both of them.

And now, long after Benson-Smith and bussing dishes at a string of Chinese restaurants, those same ears held up a felt hat with a fancy feather hatband. In the summer, it was the cooler woven straw one. You could track his comings and goings in Chinatown by that hat. He was so short and stooped that you could only find him by his hat: walking the streets, stopping to look in store windows, to peer down alleys. Or by the cloud of pipe smoke in Wing Wah Jade where he sat with the owner and thumbed the bas relief carvings on the new jade pieces.

"I used to catch da bus erryday to Chinatown. Walk around. Me, I no like stay home. Catch da bus, walk around. Chew da fat little while at da jewelry store. Den come home. Sundays, I catch bus go church. I gotta go around. No can stay home. No can now. Maybe I gotta stay home little while. Chee, I miss dat. Pretty soon maybe I can go again. Now no can.

"Now I'm alright. Maybe later I gotta go Palolo Old Man Home. But now I'm okay. Maybe one, two years from now. I donno. Ho boy, nine hundred bucks a month, you know. Dem pakes wanna cheat you, you see. Dey get anykine donations from errybody, but dey still wanna charge you nine hundred bucks a month. Ho boy."

We sat there, not looking at each other. We both looked out the window. The window screen needs cleaning, I thought. I scanned the coffee table pushed up against the corner of the living room. It was full of old photographs: his sons, his granddaughters. I found a picture of me and my brother. I must've been four or five, the "baby" of the family and had my hair slicked down and was sucking my left thumb. He complained about the weather and his arthritis.

"I'm eighty-eight years old last week. Eighty-nine, Chinese calendar. All my life I never had dis kine trouble. Now erry morning I take five pills. Damn pills cost me seventy bucks, you know. And dis damn weather . . . my arthritis . . . all sore ovah here in my shoulder and in my hands."

He stretched his fingers out wide, then closed his hand. I noticed his thumb: big and knobby and calloused still from tamping hot pipe tobacco. He wore two pieces of jade pinned to his undershirt and when we talked, he turned his good ear toward me. His earlobes bobbed and wobbled as he talked about his aches and he massaged the base of his thumb at the joint. The wind in the valley had picked up; he must've felt the rain coming. It was time to go.

*****

It was two months later after a couple of false starts and, I imagined, quite of bit of grumbling, Uncle Kam Chong made the move a couple of miles up the road to the "old man home."

Palolo Chinese Home. It was at the back of the valley where the road began to curve around and started back out again. The place was clean, plain, and functional. It was strikingly Chinese: layers of blood red paint on the columns, dark green trim and light green and white walls. There were two dormitories with upturned eaves, men's and women's, separated by a cafeteria.

It was quiet when I drove up. The men ringed the outside of their building just sitting or smoking in chairs pushed up against the walls. It was a quiet bunch. No loud talking like in Chinatown or shouting like at the mah jong games or arguing like at the fish market. Mostly everyone was just sitting outside, two or three chairs apart or inside the lounge watching TV. It looked like I was the only visitor that day. Uncle Kam Chong was sitting right outside the front door, cane in his lap, unlit pipe in his hand. He didn't recognize me until I got closer and I called out, *Kau Goong*, Uncle. How you?"

"Heh, I'm okay. I'm okay, now."

"How's this place? How's the food?"

"Not bad. Food not bad. I eat everything. Fresh air."

"Lousy," the man two seats down muttered to himself loud enough for us to hear. I looked at him and he looked away and lit a cigarette. "Same ole ting fo six years," he offered to no one in particular.

Uncle Kam Chong ignored the interruption and continued, "I eat good, eat regular. Dey no need wash my dish, I eat um so clean! So far so good, I never relax like dis before, no need worry about cook, about wash dishes. They serve you."

Another resident shuffled up and smiled at me. He pointed his cane and introduced the old timer who didn't like the food, Mr. Chun, to me. Then he introduced himself, Mr. Tam.

"Yeah," Mr. Tam said. "This is a good place. Anything you want, they get for you. The ladies very helpful." He beamed at us.

"Come watch boxing on TV," he said. He jabbed the air with his cane in the direction of the lounge.

It had started to drizzle. A light mist. Mr. Tam urged us to sit inside the lounge, "Much more comfortable and don't get wet."

Uncle pointed out that we were under the eaves.

"No, thank you," I said. "It's dry out here."

Mr. Chun muttered, "Dis only mosquito rain, rain little bit and then pau. At's all."

Mr. Tam tugged at his knitted hockey cap and pulled it down securely over his ears. Except for the cap, everyone was dressed nearly the same: bundled up in long trousers and an aloha shirt topped by a collarless, button-up sweater. Mr. Chun was one of the few who was sweaterless. Just a white tee-shirt and trousers.

"You should wear one of these hats," Mr. Tam instructed Uncle. "Keep warm."

"Yeah, maybe later on I get one," Uncle said.

"No, no just ask the ladies. They bring fo you. Free." Mr. Tam tugged again at his cap to make his point. "Free."

Mr. Tam beamed a toothless grin at me. Reassuringly he said, "This place good. Everybody is nice. You come back learn Chinese," he added as he shuffled off.

Uncle fingered his pipe. It was unlit and empty.

"Hey, you need anything. You got enough tobacco?" I asked.

"Yeah, I need tobacco. I had one big can but I donno where I put um. And matches, I need matches. I used to have some place. I donno where I put um. . . ."

"Next time I'll bring you some matches," I said.

"Yeah, one box nuff. Sometimes I forget nowdays. Ho, the other day I forget where I put my teeth. Come time to eat, I no can find um. Ho, I worry like hell. No mo teeth, no can eat, you know. Later on, somebody find um in da bathroom. Good ting. I no can remember where I left um. Drop inside da toilet, you know! Ho, da lady go soak um in solution fo me. One whole day she soak um. Otherwise, no can eat! Lucky."

"Lucky you found um," I repeated.

"Lady. Lady find um." It was Mr. Chun again. "Da lady janitor found um. Me too, sometimes forget things nowdays."

Uncle said, "One of the cafeteria ladies told me she hold my teeth for me. Whenever I need um, she bring um. 'Nah,' I told her. I no like bother."

"You gotta take care now. No lose um again. Maybe better to let the lady hold um fo you," I worried out loud.

"Hey, when you gonna take over the cafeteria?" I teased. "J'like the old days at Benson-Smith. You used to be manager or something, huh?"

"Manager, buyer, everything I was. Work there fo forty years. Start off at two dollars a week."

"A week?"

"A week. After the fourth grade, after my father died, I went work. Make some money. Help out the family. I no need too much. Only go movies now and then. Cowboy movies. Shucks.

"Pretty soon they let me run the lunch counter. Big place you know. Three hundred one time can sit down. They try anykine, you know.

They bring in all kine guys, but they no can make money. Only I could. One time they bring in three *haole* guys from the mainland to watch me fo one month because they no believe my profit so high: seventy, seventy-two, seventy-four percent. At the end of the month they ask me, 'Lee, how you do it?' I says, 'I donno.' You think I gonna tell them? Baloney! How come they ask me!"

"So how you did it, Uncle?" I asked.

"You know, only three things you gotta watch: the girls no put too much, you know, when they make samwich they put two or three slice meat. Next, watch so they no eat too much. You know, sometimes they make two, three samwich for themself and they take one, two bite then leave um alone. You see, how much waste, yeah? And den you watch, sometimes they no charge their friends or they make something big and only charge little bit. Dat's all. Dat and at the end of the month, no good have too much inventory. You order heavy at the beginning and den cut down, cut down so by the end of the month you get almost nothing. Dat's all."

"You're all right, Uncle."

"Yeah, you watch the inventory. All my meat, one size. I regulate the machine to slice, you see. One pound ham supposed to get twelve slices. Huh. And they ask me, 'How you do it, Lee?' Dey no can get seventy percent profit. When you only get forty, fifty percent that no good, you know. Something wrong."

Uncle fingered his empty pipe.

"Let's go look for your tobacco," I said. "You can show me your room."

There were four beds in each room, each corner identical with a clothes locker and small table next to the bed. Looking for the tobacco was like looking through a locker at an elementary school. Little treasures mixed in with the necessities, all conspicuously marked. My mother must've done it when he moved in. I recognized her fat, round script on every handkerchief, shirt, pants and pair of underwear. There weren't too many places to look. I stopped myself from suggesting that we go look in the community bathroom down the hall. Maybe the tobacco tin had ended up in the same place as his teeth. I found a brown paper sack full of boiled peanuts. Uncle Kam Chong offered them to me when I showed him the bag. I sniffed at it suspiciously.

"Where did you get these?" I asked.

"My friend gave me," he answered a little defensively. "One old guy. One Chinese guy. He say he know me. But I no can remember him. He know me. But I no recognize him. Ah . . ."

"When did he come?"

"Oh, couple days ago."

"Maybe you ought to give this to the kitchen. They can keep um in the icebox for you. So it doesn't spoil." I sniffed the package again.

"It's all right. No sour."

I poured a handful out. Uncle cracked one open and chewed. We settled down in the chairs right outside his room.

"So what, get activities? Things to do?"

"Yeah, they get exercise class. One lady, I donno how she know my name, she tell me, 'Eh, Mr. Lee, let's go exercise.' I say, 'No thank you, I too old.' "

"But if you exercise you sleep good, you know," I suggested.

"Hah, next day you get up, you ache all over," he laughed.

"So what, that lady your new girlfriend now?"

"Naw. I don't believe those kine now. Girlfriend. Only mouth, girlfriend. They try to skin you, boy. Danger, you know. Some of dem smooth-talker, you know." He paused to reflect and chewed on a few more peanuts.

"Well, depend on the man," he continued. "You bite, you trapped already. One time one lady tell me, 'Eh, Lee, you funny kine of man. You funny kine of man.' "

"Why she call you funny kine?"

"I donno. Maybe because I no like marry her. Shucks. You tink I damn fool?"

"Not so funny kine den, Uncle. Smart."

I poured out another handful of peanuts for him. It was slimy and white with mold.

"Aw, this is no good, Uncle," I shouted, excited and worried about the ones he had already eaten.

"It's too old, Uncle, don't eat it," I said as I swept the rest off the table into the bag. He was quiet. Like a scolded child. I looked down at his feet and I recognized my mother's round script again, "Kam Chong Lee" written across both slippers in black felt pen. They reminded me of a boxful of little girl's slippers that I had just marked with my daughter's name in preparation for school. And it all finally seemed right somehow. All of it. Uncle Kam Chong and Palolo Home and his name written across his slippers and me writing Lisa's name on hers. And the long line of toothless Chinese men and women who lived here and those yet to come. I took my place in that line and glanced down at my slippers.

I left them just the way I found them. Uncle was sitting outside, cane in his lap. Mr. Chun was smoking. Mr. Tam was waving enthusiastically from the TV room. I waved back and grinned. I'd be back.

*****

The last time I saw Uncle at Palolo Home, he was in bed, sleeping. My mother went over, called to him, and shook him awake. He was much thinner than I had remembered him.

She asked him, "You know who this is?" pointing in my direction. He turned and looked at me, not really recognizing me until she prompted him, "That's Darrell."

He turned to me and muttered, "Ho, they treat you rough ovah heah, you know. Not so easy ovah heah. Some of the new guys they treat um extra rough. But I don't say anyting. Bumbye dey learn. I donno why dey so rough."

My mother looked at me, then said to him, "Not everybody can get to be almost ninety, you know."

"Huh, not so easy being old," he grumbled. "I don't know if dey let me reach da two numbah." I didn't understand. I gave my mother a puzzled look.

"You know, when you get to ninety-one, you supposed to go church and pray. Ask if dey let you reach da two numbah . . . ninety-two. Plenny guys believe dat. Even if dey no go church. Hard to go church around heah." Next March was Uncle's ninetieth birthday, ninety-one by the Chinese calendar. My mother reassured him, "You gonna make it. No worry. You rest."

"Not so much fun being sick. Not easy, you know!"

"You pretty good today. Your nose not so runny. When you get bettah, you be all right," my mother said. "They come and take you in the wheelchair to eat, huh? Later on you can walk again by yourself to the dining room."

"Who stay Nellie's house now? The other night, I went Nellie's house sleep. Den two guys come in. I donno dem," Uncle said.

"Calvin stay Nellie's house. He live there." My mother humored him, didn't correct his mistaken notion of an overnight stay away from Palolo Home. She looked up and smiled at me.

I *could* imagine Uncle spending the night at my long-dead aunt's. It was the house that Ah Po, my grandmother, lived in her later years. I could see him in the kitchen with a cup of tea on the table. Or in the front room facing the street watching the traffic. I remembered that he went to Auntie Nellie's funeral, the last one he attended before he came to the Home. It was a big Chinese funeral. Lots of people came to see their *tsien tsang*, their teacher. Auntie Nellie had taught Chinese school for years. Probably taught them as she had taught me: behave yourself, take care of your elders, serve them tea and maybe they'll give you a *lee see*, a coin wrapped in red paper. And never, *ever* miss a funeral or *bai sahn*, the annual visit to the cemetary to pay your respects to your ancestors. Even when I was in my twenties she would praise me profusely for showing up at these occasions. No more quarters wrapped up in red paper, but she still said, "Good boy. Good boy," as if I were nine. So it seemed okay that Uncle would "spend the night" at Auntie Nellie's house.

A round-faced man walked into the room, Uncle's roommate. He wore a long-sleeved shirt and blue slacks pulled way up over a neat pot belly. He carried a cane although he really didn't seem to need it. He looked at us wide-eyed, innocent and said, "I almost drowned this morning. Yeah, the water was up to here!" He indicated neck level with his palm.

"All kinda people was here. They just walk into da room. All kine . . . Hawaiians, grandchildren, little babies. They just walk in!"

"And this machine . . ." He pointed toward the wheelchair at the foot of Uncle's bed. "I donno who ordered dis. They wheel dis ting in. I donno who brought um. Ho, da water was high! Little more I needed a boat!"

He moved over to his bed and tentatively pushed at the middle of the mattress. He looked up at us and confided, "I just testing to see if da water too deep."

My mother and I smiled at him and tried not to pay too much attention as he continued his story. Uncle complained some more about the rough treatment. I asked to take his picture.

"Nah, I no like. Too much trouble get out of bed," he said.

"No, you can stay in bed," I said. "I no mo any pictures of you and your sistah." He sat up for two shots with my mother sitting next to the bed. I snuck a closeup of him before he slid back down under the covers. We were quiet for a while, watching his eyes open and close.

"Da eye tired," my mother commented. "Da mind awake, but da eye tired."

I imagined that he was staying at Auntie Nellie's again or traveling somewhere else. No deep water or boats where Uncle was going.

The phone rang. It was my mother. "Dr. Wong just called. *Kau Goong* just passed away." I was silent.

She rattled on, "Daddy and I went to visit him yesterday. He was okay. He kept asking me when they were going to put him in the hospital. He wanted to go to the hospital. Good ting we went to see him yesterday." She laughed, "He asked for *hahm gnee*. He wasn't eating anything, just kept getting shriveled up and skinnier. And he asked for *hahm gnee*."

The pictures of my mother and Uncle Kam Chong came back today from Long's Drugs. They're not particularly good pictures. My mother and uncle have matching liver spots on the sides of their faces. Uncle is bald and my mother's hair is mostly grey and thinning. There's no mistaking that they're related. . . .

My mother has this old picture of my grandmother sitting in the middle of all her kids. All eight of them. Ah Po doesn't look much older than her eldest daughter. Everyone is in a stiff, formal pose. My mother's a little girl, maybe four or five, wearing a dress and a huge bow in her hair. Uncle Kam Chong looks around twenty. Ah Po is sitting in the middle of her brood, unsmiling. The wide Chinese-style headband across her forehead makes her look small-faced, her eyes dark and beady. She has a pale, clear complexion. . . .

There's a picture at my folks' house of me and my brother with our parents. My mother looks young and pretty. We don't ever remember our mothers that way. She's very serious. And her skin is clear, unflawed. My father is in a suit, his hair slicked back with Dixie Peach pomade. My brother is standing next to him, his hair combed in the same way. I hardly had any hair but what little I had was slicked down flat. I must have been about one or two years old, sitting on Ma's lap with a finger in my mouth. My father always points out that I was quite a thumb-sucker. They say that my brother and I look alike. I never thought so before but looking at it now, there might be some resemblance. . . .

Then there's the picture of me on my tricycle grimacing, heading full speed straight into the old Brownie. My brother must've taken that one. I wouldn't have cared if I ran him over. There's a picture of him shirtless, showing off his left bicep and making "big chest." He has this tight grin on his face, as if it were making the muscle bigger.

The lower jaw tight, the neck tense, the same mouth pulled down at the corners. There's no mistaking that we're related. No mistaking.

ABOUT THE AUTHOR AND ARTIST:
Ahta and Me

We used to hang around together at
Kawananakoa Intermediate School.

We used to wear Beatle boots and jac-shirts
and Madras plaid and P.E. shorts undah our pants
so dat we could change fast.

We used to have P.E. from Mr. Sakamoto,
who carried around one ping-pong paddle,
sandpaper one side, rubbah on da uddah side, and
he would whack your okole if you nevah take one
shower. You had choice if you was going get
whacked, though. He tell, "Sandpaper or rubbah?"

We used to have geometry from Miss Miyake
who would take your comb if she caught you
combing your hair in class. She said you could
come back after school and get um. Once I went
back for my comb, the long skinny kine dat stick
out of your back pocket, and Miss Miyake only
smile at me and pull open her desk drawer. Had
about twenty long, skinny combs greasy wit hair
and pomade and probably ukus. "Ass awright," I
told her, "I no like um back."

We used to have biology from Mr. Obata.
Ahta and me, our fish went die aftah we went
wrap um up in wet Kleenex and look at da blood
cells undah da microscope and we was doing good
until da ting went jump off da slide and go undah
da table. We went throw um back in da aquarium
real quick, but we knew dat was ours one floating

at da top when Obata went scold da class fo
putting one dead fish back in.

We used to run as soon as da bell ring to be
first in da lunch line, unless Rosa wanted to eat
lunch, den he could be first. Most times Rosa no
even stand in line. He tell somebody fo get his
lunch fo him. Da guy getting Rosa's lunch could be
first, too.

We used to arm wrestle downstairs in da
locker room. Ahta was good at arm wrestle.
Nobody could beat Ahta, even two against one.

We used to have art from Mr. Higashi cause
we wasn't in band. We made shark teet and
teardrop necklace from scrap plexiglas, ashtray and
candy dish from scrap aluminum and scrap ceramic
tiles, paperweight out of plaster of paris and scrap
rocks and shells and da small milk carton you save
from lunch, wood sculpcha out of scrap
monkeypod wood, collage out of old magazines
and scrap colored tissue. But you know what was
da most good fun?

We made pickchas of Murph da Surf on top
da desks, Ahta and me. Probably still stay dere.

Darrell H.Y. Lum